KONDRATIEV

PIONEER OF THE BUSINESS CYCLE

KONDRATIEV

PIONEER OF THE BUSINESS CYCLE

FREDERIC WEEKES

iUniverse, Inc.
Bloomington

KONDRATIEV
PIONEER OF THE BUSINESS CYCLE

iUniverse books may be ordered through booksellers or by contacting:

iUniverse
1663 Liberty Drive
Bloomington, IN 47403
www.iuniverse.com
1-800-Authors (1-800-288-4677)

ISBN: 978-1-4759-5199-8 (sc)
ISBN: 978-1-4759-5200-1 (ebk)

Printed in the United States of America

iUniverse rev. date: 09/28/2012

TABLE OF CONTENTS

NOTES ON
NICOLAI DMITRI KONDRATIEV

The Russian economist's name can be spelled in different ways but the rendition above is sufficiently accurate to allow an investigator to locate the gentleman in an encyclopedia. His dates are 1882 to 1938.

Kondratiev was educated in the university at St. Petersburg. He learned statistics as well as economics. When the Bolsheviks came to power in 1917, Kondratiev joined the regime in the economic section where he focused on agriculture, contributing to the five-year plans.

His interest in the business cycle over the long term established his reputation and contributed to his demise. He fell victim to one of Stalin's purges in 1938. Kondratiev found that the business cycle lasted approximately fifty years, from one major depression to the next, as an example. He did not find data going further back than the time of Napoleon (Emperor of the French from 1804 to 1815). Each of these repetitive periods has been given the name 'wave.' About four 'waves' have transpired since the start of Kondratiev's data gathering.

The graph on the last page of part 17 is representative but fictional as are the six important moments and periods that are identified. Most anyone who reflects on events since the Great

Depression will find the graph and the important moments satisfactory if not absolutely accurate.

The main purpose of writing this book is to suggest that the situations we live through are inevitable if you believe Kondratiev's data and conclusions. He felt that it did not matter a great deal who was in office, the 'waves' kept coming.

While at the University of Pennsylvania, I attended classes at the Moore School of Electrical Engineering. I knew that across the campus was a different place called the Wharton School. On reflection I might have been better prepared to write this book had I studied at Wharton.

A second purpose in writing this book is to express opinions gathered over the years. As the reader will determine, I have become a man of the Right and it gives me pleasure to chide the Left when appropriate.

Kondratiev's downfall, more than likely, came about because he advocated that savings programs should precede manufacturing. An enterprise, be it the state or a private organization, should build up reserves to pay for the manufacturing cycle: As an example, if tractors were to be manufactured, factories should be constructed; machinery purchased; workers hired and trained; etc. Surely these activities were viewed as capitalistic notions. One guesses further that his name appeared on a long list of individuals to be executed and that Stalin, without reading the list and giving it his best consideration, simply placed his initials at the bottom of the last page.

There is a new four-volume set of some of Kondratiev's works. Look to Amazon for price and availability for this set and other works by Kondratiev.

Kondratiev, when analyzing long waves, used the seasons to indicate the various activities taking place. He identified them as spring, summer, autumn and winter. In this text we have moved from four to six periods and we call them: Decline, Recovery, Steady State, Enthusiasm, Euphoria, Burst Bubble, and back to Decline. We feel that there is more meaning in the six names selected than in the four seasons.

All characters in this piece with the exception of Kondratiev are fictional.

WAVES IN OUR LIVES

WAVES IN OUR LIVES
PART 1

Rob Doran had followed what he felt was a straight line in life: the expected pre-college schooling, then four years at university, followed by leaving town to earn a PhD in economics before returning. The dean at his first school emphasized the value of obtaining advanced degrees at another university than one's own, the value being to learn the different points of view expressed by other professors, some of whom would become career-long associates. The advice proved invaluable.

Doran's father, a GI, had met a woman wearing the American uniform while stationed in England. The exact schedule was not discussed, whether marriage or pregnancy came first, but this member of the Women's Army Corps and Doran's father paired off in 1944 and were only separated at death, which arrived for both husband and wife in their early eighties.

Doran's mother had read *Robinson Crusoe* and was impressed by the scrapes the young seafarer got himself into, only to survive them and prosper. She was determined to produce a son and name him Robinson. She had told her husband that there were too many Arthurs and Alices in his family already, they having discussed the names of a few relatives. Her husband was not allowed to participate in selecting a name for the arrival, be it male or female. Robinson Doran was born in an Army hospital in

England and dispatched to the United States late in 1945 in a ship crammed with war brides and a few brand new citizens. Doran's advancement through the teaching ranks was not spectacular except for his authorship of a textbook on finance that became one of the standards adopted by business schools throughout the nation. From that effort there came to him prestige and cash. There were four editions over twenty years. He never tired of hearing his text referred to by his last name. Among a certain group of intellectuals he had become a household name.

Rob had met Rose at a local all-girls college when they were undergraduates. They were attending a mixer, one of those events in which people of the opposite sex spend an evening dancing, talking and evaluating. Young men and women would not attend unless they were expecting action to result, not that evening necessarily, but in the weeks to come. Rob always wondered whether part of his attraction to Rose was her resemblance to his mother. She was pretty, beautifully built (*stacked* was the expression in use at the time), and quick.

He had formulated a theory over the years concerning Rose's brains. Rob felt that the average brain contained the same number of neurons as an excellent brain, but that in the excellent brain the neurons were aligned, as crops would be in a well-tended vegetable garden. They would not be scattered randomly. His theory held that the reading of important texts on Rose's part eliminated the scattering effect that was at work in most brains. Rob loved Rose's brains and her body. The order might vary from day to day. He never tired of discussing important matters with her, nor did they ever tire of passionate moments.

2008 had been a dramatic year for Rose and Rob and for half of the American population as well. The values of their investments and their house fell. They felt fortunate that their house was paid for. The value of the farm, as they called it (it was situated west of the city), may have gone down but there was no effect on their lives. Rob had used his inheritance from his father (his mother had died first) to purchase acreage west of the city, on the way to Lancaster, perhaps two-thirds of the way. There were over ten acres and a stream ran through the property. Part of it was wooded and Rob thought he could make out the outlines of an apple orchard, perhaps planted during the Depression and abandoned after the war when the owners departed for the city. That's how Rob imagined the chronology of events leading up to his purchase. He did not meet with a non-resident-owner but negotiated through a real estate broker. The place was situated less than a mile from a town. Rob also thought of the words *village* and *hamlet* for the collection of three stores and a gas station. The road from the town to his place was paved halfway, turned to gravel, and went on to other farms, all occupied presently but only a few worked.

Rob and Rose never agreed on the purchase. Rose's point was that it wouldn't see much use as they were city folks, enmeshed with friends and activities. Rob had always been the one over the last decade to plan weekends in the country. Rose threw herself into making habitable the house on the place. The setting was perfect, on a slight rise with a view of the creek. There was no lawn. The land from the house to the creek held shrubs and grass and a sprinkling of small trees. In addition to the house where they stayed, there was a small house, something between a small house and a tool shed. They called it The Shack.

The originators of the house, perhaps two hundred years back, had excavated a cellar and lined the walls with stone. That person, or another occupant later on, had put in a cement floor and attempted to make the walls watertight.

Above the stone basement only wood had been used. Downstairs consisted of a kitchen, dining room, and main room. Upstairs had three rooms as well: a bathroom and two bedrooms. Rob and Rose noticed right away that a recent owner had been born pessimistic. The bathroom had a gas water heater while the kitchen had one operated by electricity. There was an electric stove and a gas contraption that could be used to boil water. The large room downstairs had a fireplace, a gas stove, and two portable electric heaters.

Rose's contribution was to find furniture that complemented the style of the house and its location. There were antique stores to visit where the appropriate pieces could be purchased. After injecting her knowledge ("That's what any woman would do," she told Rob.) she started to care about the place to the extent that she added curtains to hide the venetian blinds and covered the pillows and cushions in the large room with quiet green and brown materials.

When Rose had finished her tasks around the house she became reluctant to leave her home in the city. Philadelphia was home as it always had been. There was a first time when Rob went to the country alone. He claimed his gardening activities could not be delayed. Spring was on the way and he had to clear and till the soil before he planted. When he drove off for the four days, they parted on friendly terms but that could be accounted for by their many years together. Rose felt that his new view on how he should spend his life would go away. Rob wasn't a farmer and soon enough he would fall into agreement with his wife on how to spend his time in retirement. She advised that he return to a life of the mind: reading, researching and writing. He had reached retirement age and decided on winding up his affairs at the university sometime during 2009.

WAVES IN OUR LIVES
PART 2

The end of 2008 will be remembered as the time when governments everywhere went into action to revive their respective economies. The little country of Iceland had over-borrowed and found itself in trouble. Many other countries were navigating in choppy waters. Unemployment increased, some people stopped paying on their mortgages, others on their credit cards or car loans. Banks were having difficulties identifying persons or companies that were certain to repay money advanced to them.

Rob's stated and written solution to the crisis had two parts. The first was to eliminate the federal tax on corporate income for three years. The cost to the Treasury would be three hundred billion dollars per year, about the amount of the stimulus package. The second part would be to permit the geniuses that had caused the problems with the economy to stay in place and repair the damages they had created. Who could know more about the corrupt practices that created havoc in the financial sector than those very executives who created the problems? Rob would advance these ideas to fellow professors, many of whom subscribed to the concepts, but only half-heartedly. They needed time to consider all this, they would say. The professors he would engage in conversation who were not in his field were also lukewarm, their hang-up being that they were accustomed to corporations paying taxes, that corporations had plenty of money, and that they, the fat cats as they called them, shouldn't get a free pass for three years when the rest of us continued paying into the Treasury. Most of them, however, admitted that Rob's version of the stimulus would be more effective than the version already passed by Congress and signed into law.

Rob's best friend was in the engineering faculty. He understood solid state physics, microcircuits, and electronics in general. He had been recruited from a semiconductor firm to join the faculty, being one of many engineers who had earned a PhD in either physics or electrical engineering. His name was Vince Williams, originally from Minnesota. Vince and Rob were of the same age, give or take a few months. They had both served in Vietnam. Their friendship was based on that, and on being neighbors (three blocks). They each had two children. Vince was always willing to listen to Rob as he went on with his political views. Vince's patience came naturally to him. He understood what Rob was saying while he knew that Rob would understand little of what he told him about technical advances. Once when Rob asked Vince why he was so generous in his listening habits, Vince answered that at least he, Vince, was learning as he listened while Rob was going over material he already knew and therefore was not expanding his horizons as he spoke.

Vince had lost his wife three years previously and had not found a new love interest. When Rob mentioned this shortage in Vince's life to Rose one day, he was taken aback when she commented, "I think he wants to have sex with me. That is, he's always wanted to have sex with me. Women sense these things." There ensued a question and answer period about the signals Rose was receiving. She maintained that it came down to eye contact and had first surfaced two decades ago when the couples spent a weekend together on the Atlantic shore. From that time forward, Vince had always transmitted to Rose an extra interest, a slight urgency, but never supported the message in conversation. Rose assumed that Vince knew he did not need to add words. This situation did not upset the friendship between the men, although Rob kept in mind the desire for his wife on Vince's part, particularly now that he was planning to spend time in the country, in all likelihood without the company of Rose. Rob wondered who might make the first move, if either one did. In any event, Rob did not change his plans to spend time in the country at their place.

As the government was making plans to spend the money in the stimulus package, Rob would remark to associates that no one had telephoned him yet. He said it with a smile on his face, but at the core he had half-expected that one of the members of the new White House entourage would ask for his opinions. He knew most of them. One had taken classes from him. Rob was well-known, but it must be said that he was of the other political party than the one in office.

Had anyone contacted him, he would have made the point that terminating the federal tax on corporate earnings would inject cash immediately into any company that was profitable. With fresh cash, companies could pay off debt, thereby reducing the drain of interest payments; start new programs in R&D, or marketing, or sales, and improve manufacturing; and most important, hire new people to fill the positions required. Rob would quip to his friends that his program was too simple to grasp. The power brokers in Washington would look for complex solutions. As it turned out, they, those in office, viewed the economic slowdown as a chance to make major changes in environmental policy, health care, education, transportation, and so on. A popular quote coming out of the White House was that a crisis provided opportunities too good to turn down. Rob knew he didn't have the quotation word for word, but that was the gist of it.

Those in power, including the Congress, rode off in all directions at once,[1] spending billions and accomplishing little. Rob sensed that hard times could come and be visited upon the country for at least ten years. At his age, he might very well complete the roundtrip, from dust to dust, before good times returned.

The undergirding of this belief was simple, that the government was overburdened with debt. In 1929, when the market slid, the national debt was between two and four billion dollars. He didn't recall exactly and couldn't verify the sum as most tables started with the year 1940. At the end of President Roosevelt's second term, in the winter of 1940, the national debt had grown to fifty-seven billion dollars. Currently the debt was at ten trillion, or some such astronomical amount. With the government on the hook, through social security and Medicare for additional trillions, with debt way beyond the moon, perhaps reaching out past the solar system, the government was headed for bankruptcy. For this reason, Rob was cultivating his ten or so acres.

---

[1]   Stephen Leacock, in his 1911, *Nonsense Novels*, wrote as follows: "He flung himself from the room, flung himself upon his horse, and rode madly off in all directions."

FREDERIC WEEKES

Rob, as an investor, had always selected corporations that carried little or no debt. He imagined that a CEO running a company carrying massive debt would wake up each morning wondering how he would come up with the cash to make the interest payment on the debt, and on occasion, when it came due, how to handle maturing principal without substituting new debt.

CEOs of debt-free companies, on the other hand, woke up wondering about the development of new products or the success of a new advertising campaign. Rob guessed that one of the preoccupations in Washington for years to come would be to make certain to collect sufficient money in taxes to pay the interest on the national debt because any shortage there would bring borrowing to a halt. The Treasury could conduct auctions of fresh instruments of debt but no one might attend the auctions. Interest on the debt was the second largest item in the budget, after Defense, and Rob guessed that soon enough interest on the debt would replace Defense as the largest item.

12

WAVES IN OUR LIVES
PART 3

Rose kept a calendar for the year in the kitchen. She kept a red felt pen on the counter and marked off each day as she prepared dinner. She would write in their social engagements, using a ballpoint pen from a collection lying in a plastic tray. A telephone mounted on the wall completed the equipment for what Rose regarded as their office. She ran their lives from this corner of the kitchen. The breakfast table was nearby. She could place the family checkbook on it and pay the monthly bills.

One day, Rob removed the calendar from its nail and placed it on the breakfast table and studied it before selecting a week late in March. "How about these five days?" he asked Rose.

"Will you be back for the weekend?" she answered.

"Yes, and how will you occupy yourself while I'm gone?"

"I have reading and projects and I can always telephone a friend to go to a movie. And spur of the moment things come up."

"Will you be lonely?"

"Some. How about you?"

"I'll be lonely, but tired if I exert myself, and I have neighbors, all of whom you know."

"I've put together a CARE package for you but didn't do anything about wine."

"I'll stop at the store on the way and fuel up. No more than a half-bottle per night and nothing for lunch."

"It's a good policy, Robby," she said.

He packed his car, kissed Rose, and said he would telephone her on arrival and each evening save Friday when he would be on the road. It had been two years since they had given in to modern ways, and decided that each should have a cell phone. Their two children were surprised.

Rob was of the school that most everything was to be measured. It was sixty-seven miles from home to the place in the country, one way, and he could make it on two gallons. Four gallons for the roundtrip. He had bought this small, high mileage car two years previously and it had reshaped his life, making it impossible to transport great amounts of cargo. He had to keep most of what he needed at the place in the country and limit himself to carting clean clothes and the food Rose selected for him. This would be his first five-day foray into the country.

His principal duty was to decide where to plant vegetables and fruit trees. Potatoes would be his anchor, followed by corn and beans. He would store the potatoes in the basement and learn to can corn and the vegetables. His neighbors knew how to can and certainly they would show him how. Fruits were a different matter. He had heard that you planted apple trees, then spliced in what you wanted in the way of a crop. From the first planting to sinking your teeth into the fruit required five years, he had read. He liked peaches and plums but had no idea whether they grew successfully this far north, nor did he know the wait for the first crop. "Learn by doing," he said to himself.

Rob knew that a football field, not counting the end zones, was about an acre. A field might be fifty yards wide and no doubt a hundred yards long. Converting yards to feet, a football field was 300 feet long and 150 feet wide, and multiplying those figures gave 45,000 square feet. An acre consisted of about 44,000 square feet, he didn't know exactly, so he had a property that consisted of a bit more than ten football fields. One-half acre would be more than he needed for potatoes, corn and vegetables. He decided he would grow all he could eat on a half acre. Maybe he'd have a vegetable stand, or sell his surplus to the grocery store. It was good to know that he could can three hundred meals and store them in the basement on shelves he would design and build: beets, carrots, peas, string beans, lima beans, a feast every day. All that food, but what about protein? He would have to plant trees that gave walnuts, hazelnuts and almonds. Perhaps an additional half-acre would be required. He reflected that his mother had reasoned correctly when she named him Robinson, after Crusoe.

The idea of having animals crossed his mind but he did not want the responsibility of milking and feeding them. He might get a dog if he moved out to the country, but steer clear of cows, goats and chickens. Some of his neighbors could swap milk and butter in exchange for canned tomatoes and peaches. In the first years he might be required to buy peaches to can. Meat and fish remained a problem, as did coffee, tea and sugar, and of course red wine. In the world he imagined, these would still be available at the store. They would be in limited supply and expensive, but he would cut back and manage.

He questioned the idea of deer. They looked so innocent and harmless. Perhaps they were. But they would eat his plantings down to the ground. He would need stout fencing, which, of course, would cost plenty. He believed in the division of labor and could see that he would be required to have his garden area fenced in by experts. He could not do it himself. How high can deer jump? The people who install fences would know.

Rob's nearest neighbors were the Gunthers. They were a couple in their middle sixties that had moved from the city some ten years ago. They did not move for the reason that Rob did (the world as we know it is coming to an end) but they came in order to get away from the high population density of New Jersey. They had experienced all the difficulties that Rob was confronting as he toyed with making the move from city to country. They grew their own food, cut wood for the fireplace, made clothes from cloth they bought, and started a business of making wood objects such as salad bowls that they sold through a store in Lancaster.

As ten-year survivors, they had ample wisdom to share with newcomers. Because they had been city people who had relocated to the woods of eastern Pennsylvania, it seemed strange to Rob that they had given up most city manners and gravitated toward being Ma and Pa, with long dresses for her and bib overalls for him. Perhaps that's what ten years in the country does to you. They were pleasant and welcoming to Rob, as well as being informative. They would not force their opinions or their ways on Rob. They were generous with what they had learned of life in the country. Rob acknowledged to himself that while he had owned property on that road for ten years, the Gunthers had lived their lives as his neighbors and had farmed all along for those same years. Rob knew they were far more advanced than he was in making their way without the support that living in a city with a healthy bank balance offers a person.

The Gunthers were church-going persons. Rose and Rob had long since severed their ties to the Almighty, but Rob, for the first time, gathered that people come to church on Sundays to form support groups. It's when adversity strikes that people need what others have to offer. He wondered where the Gunthers went on Sunday mornings. What would be their denomination? Rose and Rob had been married in Rose's family garden by a Methodist clergyman who did not object to working outside his church. Since the wedding, neither had ever entered a religious building except to admire the inside of a Gothic cathedral in Europe. No doubt the Gunther's church would be plain, made of wood, and painted white. He would ask them subtly about churches in the area, as though he attended regularly at home.

It appeared to Rob that the year 2009 would be difficult for many. Unemployment nationwide had moved above 10% and although the Dow had advanced to ten thousand, many investors, with good reason, were undecided whether seven thousand was not its true level. When Rob made it home Friday evening at the end of his five days in the country, he sensed coolness immediately in Rose's attitude. She may be disapproving of his interest in their place in the country or maybe that rascal Vince had been by to steal a kiss. Rob knew it would work out in the end because when society unraveled, as it would in the year following, the place in the country would be more appealing than city life and Rose would join him, praising him for his foresight.

WAVES IN OUR LIVES
PART 4

Forty-eight hours passed before the tensions between Rose and Rob faded away. He tried to find the cause but Rose was not forthcoming. Rob concluded that Rose could not bring herself to agree that planting one foot in the countryside, way beyond the city, was a sensible thing to do in the event most of the institutions in the nation collapsed. Her point of view was that the current situation would stabilize and that normal times would return far sooner than Rob thought. "You're being dramatic, Robby," she had said. "We have this enormous momentum, three hundred million people all working to improve things. That's lots of people, as big as a tidal wave," she added.

She had heard his sermon on the debt that the federal government had to manage and agreed that it was a heavy load but did not think it would break the bank. "Other countries have carried larger debts per capita than we're carrying now, so while I'm worried, I'm not panicking." Those few words summed up her attitude. Rob, on the other hand, would prattle on, using ten times the number of paragraphs she used in an attempt to prove Rose wrong. He never succeeded.

"Such a pessimist. This crisis is taking place in a field you know something about. That's why you have so much to say. I don't hear a peep out of you on climate change." That was a taunt, of course, and Rob, feeling his temper rise, said, "Maybe your pal Vince can make the case to you on dealing with carbon dioxide." Rob's answer to Rose was not farfetched, as Vince had fallen back on his ample technical knowledge to explain to both of them the elements at work that could increase the temperature of the earth's atmosphere.

Rose and Rob did not carry on arguments. This exchange approximated the normal duration and Rob realized right away that his introducing Vince the way he did revealed an insecurity he held that Rose did not suspect. Of course, when he said the words, he knew she would go back to her statement that Vince wanted to have sex with her and had wanted it for two decades.

Forty-eight hours after his return they were lovers again. Sunday was warm and had the feel of the first day of spring. They worked in their garden that afternoon, discussing what they would plant. Their minds went away from the world coming to an end forcing them out to the country. At sunset, they came in, poured wine, and moved upstairs. Among other things, Rob said, "We threw away Friday and Saturday nights."

While they didn't discuss it, Rob continued thinking about his planting program. He would make a tentative plan and present it to the Gunthers. That went for the fence as well. The Gunthers had a fence.

Rob thought he could spend four days in the country over a weekend and get to know the Gunthers. He did know they were Emil and Mary. He would leave early on a Friday morning, spend Saturday, Sunday and Monday in the country, and return Tuesday morning. If he did this in the first week of April he could break ground on his vegetable garden, find out about seeds, and turn over a little soil with a spade. He had decided against investing in a gasoline-driven device. It didn't appear to be the appropriate thing to do when the supply of gasoline could dry up. If he were sufficiently diplomatic he could elicit a fair amount of advice from the Gunthers on farming and go to church with them as well.

The availability of the Gunthers fell into his lap. After he had pulled into his front yard and taken in his two loads from the car to the kitchen, his telephone rang.

"This is Emil Gunther. You're back sooner than I thought you might be." They chatted a bit and Emil asked Rob if he could come over for supper at six o'clock. "It will be simple but the missus will give you plenty."

Rob was surprised that Emil and Mary knew a fair amount about him. Over the years they had spoken a few times and Rose could have had extensive conversations with Mary. Emil Gunther was a retired high school math teacher and Mary had been a librarian in an elementary school. They had retired at the same time and executed their plan, a long-cherished dream of living the simple life in the country.

It did not take long for the conversation to turn to the current crisis as Emil knew that Rob had been a professor of finance. "How do you see it?" Emil asked.

"Many places to start. One is that no one's in charge. You have several heavyweights in the White House, and then Treasury, followed by the Federal Reserve, topped off by both houses of Congress. There might be a couple of hundred important people to satisfy, with the result that finger-pointing becomes the most popular activity."

"I've read that the president meets every day with his top brass. That should reduce the number of people in the loop."

"Certainly it does but the others need to be consulted on the important points."

"See what you mean," Emil said. "What do you do about the too many people?"

"Appoint a committee of three with executive powers. You know about the mortgages, don't you?" Rob asked.

"Well, vaguely. Good ones and bad ones mixed together," Emil answered.

"It's surprising that those bundles of mortgages haven't been sorted yet. There are not an infinite number of them. The government buys them and goes to work. The performing mortgages are golden. They're easy to sell. The non-performing ones represent a house on a piece of land. The owner of the mortgage owns the property. Auction it off. If the auction brings in more than the value of the mortgage, the balance goes to the person who bought the property."

"Pretty simple. Why don't they do that?"

"They may get around to it," Rob said, "but remember they have to get approval from a couple of hundred players."

"See what you mean," Emil said.

Mary called the men to the table. "You can finish settling scores and eat your soup at the same time."

Rob had only an audience of two, three counting himself, but once wound up he found it difficult to break off. "To make things worse, they have a new accounting practice. It's called mark-to-market and you can tell from its name that anyone holding an asset, as a bank does, has to value the asset for what it's worth in the market. So a bank holds a three hundred thousand dollar mortgage on a property in the area where the price of all real estate falls, then the value of this asset must be marked down with all the rest. Enough of this and the bank's capitalization is insufficient and the regulators prod the bank into selling stock or getting an infusion of capital somehow."

"I would think that with things as they are, this mark-to-market would harm plenty of businesses, banks included," Emil said.

"Well, sure enough. They'll change it someday, back to what it was, but when you adjust to market, do it slowly. None of that precipitous stuff," Rob answered.

Rob changed the subject. He asked Mary, "I've seen you driving out of here Sunday mornings. Must be off to church, I'd guess."

"You guessed right. We're Lutherans. Emil's family came over from Germany and there you're either Lutheran or Catholic. The church is easy to find. You go up to the store, turn right and go about two miles. It's on the left side of the road."

After supper, Mary cleared the table and the three of them discussed how Rob could get started as a gardener with the objective of breaking loose from the city and living as independently as possible in the country.

"Do you think Rose will come out here to live?" Mary asked.

"Right now the answer is no, but as the economy crumbles and life in the city becomes increasingly difficult she might change her mind. We'll know at harvest time," Rob said and smiled.

They discussed the vegetables that he should grow, where to buy seed, how to plant potatoes, how far apart to place seeds and the difficulty of starting an orchard. Mary appeared to Rob to be more knowledgeable than Emil. She was the one of the two who had managerial skills. They ended the evening with a tour of the basement where Rob saw the results of hard work, just what he hoped to accomplish. Mary must be an expert preserver of what they had grown.

"We have plenty, about a year's worth. You don't need more than that. If Rose doesn't move with you, you'll only need to plant and put up half of what you see here, if that," Mary advised him.

On Sunday, before nine-thirty, Rob was at the Gunther's car. Emil drove and Mary explained that there was a collection as part of the service and that most everyone gave a bit more as they went through the line in the parish hall for coffee and cookies after the service.

The minister was middle aged and articulate. The words Rob remembered dealt with the good fortune enjoyed by the members. They had put to work the bounty found in the soil and had enough to be able to give to those less fortunate than themselves.

Rob found it a simple matter to concentrate on the service, aided as they were by prayer books and hymnals. Rob found the experience pleasurable, perhaps made so by the opportunity to glance at the unattached women. They could be married with their men at home, or they could be single: widowed, divorced, or not married. He didn't see anyone he yearned to talk to after the service, during the coffee hour, but he knew it was never obvious. The ones meant for you came concealed any number of ways.

Mary introduced Rob to eight or ten people, those standing near. Perhaps some moved near to be introduced as he guessed he was the only stranger in the room. He found them welcoming and soft-spoken. From what they said, each was at a different stage in making the transition from city to country. Rob didn't think he met any natives.

This was the first time in Rob's life that he sensed that churchly fabric was part of society. Any person among the hundred or so in the hall would come to the aid of a wounded person among them. It was personal and limited to those in similar circumstances as they. He had never felt that the members of the faculty club would be concerned if a colleague fell, beyond an expression of sympathy. In the city, there were organizations to take care of you if misfortune struck.

Rob didn't think the people in the room were brought together by a belief in the Almighty. He thought they knew that they needed one another. He wondered whether Rose and he had shortchanged themselves and their children by keeping this cohesive social experience at a distance.

WAVES IN OUR LIVES
PART 5

Rob could not deny the difficulties of the situation he found himself in. He and Rose and a million or two people in Philadelphia would make it through the crisis, even if it lasted ten years. Human beings are resourceful and resilient and while times would test everyone in the country, there wouldn't be mass starvation or civil war. There might be riots but Rob believed that they would be of short duration and generally not violent.

What would happen to their marriage, Rob wondered? It would not endure with Rose in the city and he living in the country, one driving sixty-seven miles to be with the other. Rob knew Rose to be more independent than that. She would exit the marriage and move in another direction rather than lead a half-life, even with the person she had been married to for over forty years.

Rob recognized a stubborn streak in himself that had always been off to the side. For some reason he could not get it out of his head that he was correct, that the world as he knew it was coming to an end. He had not met another person who shared his view. The Gunthers were not as pessimistic as he was, nor were any members of his faculty, nor any of their friends. Most people he knew, and therefore who knew his views, humored him and quietly pitied Rose. "He'll come to his senses when none of his fears materialize," they would say.

The summer of 2009 progressed as Rob had guessed it might. National unemployment passed 9% by Labor Day. The first signs of inflation appeared as food prices went up, imported foods such as coffee and cocoa moving up more than wheat, corn and dairy products. Income went down because there were no pay raises to compensate for inflation. Rob's pension fund had been hit as markets staggered but Rob's monthly check was still for the same amount. The Dow had found a new home at eight thousand.

Rob was spending half his time in the country. He and Rose were existing at a lower level of conviviality than they ever had. Rob had extended the invitation, which Rose refused. "I will not live in the country. I prefer taking my chances right here, starving if it comes to that."

In September, she brought up the matter of Vince. The two of them had talked on the telephone during Rob's absence. They were social conversations, Rose said, each asking how the other was managing. On one occasion Rose had invited Vince to dinner. She said they were both lonely. He came in carrying a bottle of wine. After going through half of it, Vince said, "I'm keeping my clothes on. As soon as I undo one button, Rob will come bounding through that door, claiming you, admitting that he was wrong all along, that he could see signs that the world was patching itself together." Rose smiled and answered, "I admire your restraint. I'm keeping my clothes on also."

The remainder of the evening, as Rose recounted it to Rob, was spent as one between two old friends. When they were at the door, Rose permitted Vince to kiss her once on the lips, the first time between them. Rose did not mind tormenting Rob in repayment for the anxiety he had caused her.

Rob had been successful in his garden. Once the harvest came in he would return with far more than the two of them could eat. They gave the surplus to neighbors. Rob was busy canning for the winter as he had been taught by the Gunthers. He sensed that the contents of his basement would carry him through the winter. He also sensed that his marriage would come to an end once it became obvious that he intended to spend the winter in the country.

When he decided to make the move, at the end of September, and brought it up to Rose, she said, "Well, it's obvious you've been leaning that way. When you make your move, you should know that we're no longer married, no matter what the documents say, and you may as well know that I don't plan to live here alone. I'll sleep with Vince, become his lover, and move in with him, if that's what he wants."

"You've already discussed this with Vince?"

"No, but there's no sense in having two people living alone, lonely, in half-empty houses, when we could be living sensible lives together."

"He'll finally get his wish," Rob said.

"Yes, and if I moved there this house could go to Harriet. She must be tired of living in an apartment with her husband and a growing child."

There it was, his life brought down by the economic follies of others. Without the crisis he would never have taken seriously a need to move to the country. The purchase of the place ten years previously was the result of a back-to-nature longing that he did not comprehend. It had nothing to do with leaving Rose. It was a natural desire he had had since childhood.

On his way out to the country, Rob thought about how he would do his laundry. It embarrassed him that he worried about such mundane aspects of his life just when he had lost his wife. He knew the Gunthers had a washing machine but preferred drying their clothes on a line behind the house. Rob decided that he would ask the Stewards who lived next door in the opposite direction from the Gunthers, therefore away from the village. The negotiation of laundry in exchange for something he had that they wanted would be interesting. It would be his first experiment with barter. He had heard that a fair amount of bartering was taking place and assumed that it would be on the increase.

On arrival he unpacked his car, which he had filled with books, clothes and alcoholic beverages. He wasn't sure how to organize his life, what with the winter coming. The cold weather would keep him indoors but he could make a routine of walking to the village to check his mail at the post office, which was located in the rear of the store. The wife of the husband and wife team that owned the store was the postmaster and she knew all about the people in the area who came in to check their mail boxes. If there was any interesting mail she would already have studied the postmark, the return address, and the handwriting. One day she said to Rob, "Nothing today except you got a letter from your son. Often times they ask for money." The exchange went on. "Where was it postmarked?" Rob asked. "Chestnut Hill, that's where he lives, isn't it?" "Yes, he just wants to wish me well and wonder how his mother will do without me." "Well, that's settled then. She's not spending the winter with you."

"No, she might move in with Vince Williams. He's been in here. He's a widower my age. They've always been a fallback for one another." Rob knew that if he gave gossip he would get back more than he gave.

With that exchange finished, Rob was certain that the inhabitants of the village would know within a day or two about Rob's arrival for the winter and the end of his marriage to Rose. This form of dissemination of the news saved Rob a fair amount of time. In addition, if there were a woman interested in him she might calculate how to get into his crosshairs without too much difficulty.

Rob decided that he would start the day with breakfast and news on the radio. This would be followed by an inspection of the property if it was not raining or snowing. He would look for tracks from deer and when it snowed for footprints of bear, which he never found. He would gather limbs that had fallen and take to the house any branch that could be burned in the fireplace. He walked to the village everyday after the mail arrived. In the afternoon he thought he would read, mostly fiction, but occasionally the journals from his professional societies. He was surprised how easy it was to let go of the elements of his career. He would have to find a hobby that pleased and satisfied him. Painting could be the answer. He had read that Gilbert Stewart had painted George Washington perhaps a hundred times, from memory except for the early executions when Washington may have sat for him. He thought there would be a market for portraits of past presidents. There were photographs of Lincoln and he knew you could buy photographs of the bust of Jefferson done by Houdon, that French sculptor who crossed the Atlantic for the express purpose of capturing in marble Jefferson, Franklin and other notables.

Rob and Rose had made many friends through bridge although they had never graduated to tournament play. If he let it out on the wire that he was interested in playing, there was little doubt that he would be asked to complete a foursome. All that was required was a hint dropped at the postmaster's.

WAVES IN OUR LIVES
PART 6

It had been on Rob's mind that he would get back to his work on Kondratiev. He knew it to be a serious interest as all his papers on the subject were with him in the country. He had come across this Russian economist during his doctoral studies and had always been interested in him. Kondratiev was not the only economist to track business cycles but he may have been the most important as the term *Kondratiev Waves* exists while no other economist's name is so closely identified with the business cycle.

When examining any of Kondratiev's waves, Rob found them to be graphs with time in years along the horizontal axis and various measurable phenomena on the vertical axis. Some of these might be the GDP of a nation, or wages, costs of commodities and volume of production such as barrels of oil and tons of steel. Kondratiev found that the bottoms of waves (depressions) were separated by fifty to sixty years. Of course, the peaks (the good times) were separated by about the same number of years as well.

Kondratiev had gone back to Napoleonic times and forward from there to the mid-years of Stalin's reign. Stalin and the Bolsheviks in power disapproved of Kondratiev's findings as they thought that the planned economies of Communist countries would not exhibit waves. There would be a constant upward path in production, or so those in charge guessed.

Kondratiev was out of favor during most of the time that followed the Revolution of 1917. He was sent to prison in 1930 and his execution was ordered by Stalin in 1938. Nicolai Dmitrievich Kondratiev was born in 1892 and had served the state in several capacities from the time the Bolsheviks came to power in 1917.

In Rob's text, which was used by many schools that taught economics and finance, Rob had allocated a chapter to business cycles and Kondratiev. As a result, many graduate students across the country were familiar with that Russian's work.

Rob had always wanted to tie in Kondratriev's findings with the psychology of human beings, not simply to economic data. Rob thought it would be a normal progression. He thought that people at some points in their lives would be depressed and therefore feel negatively on their country's prospects, as he was presently. This same group could not remain depressed for ever and Rob reasoned that they would graduate into the first sensations of optimism. From there it would only be a matter of time before they would be singing "Happy Days Are Here Again." That mood would last until a fair segment of the population became exuberant, and at that moment the first sign of excesses would appear in the system. The scoundrels and manipulators would gain access to power for the sake of filling their pockets; then it would only be a matter of time before the system could no longer function. The nation would once again fall into depression. Perhaps sixty years would have passed. Rob always thought that the psychology of the population, taken cumulatively, was the driving force behind the business cycle.

Kondratiev never coupled the behavior of humans to the steps in his wave theory. Human beings, however, manufactured more or less steel, planted and harvested more and less wheat, accounted for increases and decreases in GDP, and so on. The behavior of humans should be part of the theory. Kondratiev went so far as to assert that the national savings rate had to go up in order to provide capital to expand the manufacture of capital goods. No doubt he was thinking of tractors, locomotives, steel rails, cement and fertilizer. Why couldn't the connection be made between human behavior and the Kondratiev wave? It could have been this emphasis on the saving rate that got Kondretiev in trouble with the Communists. The idea of the need for savings to make expansion of the economy possible was certainly a capitalistic concept. Rob thought that if he could tie in human nature with the Kondratiev wave there would be additional recognition for Kondratiev and possibly a prize or a commendation of sorts for him. He had pondered the puzzle over the years and discussed it with Rose and occasionally with Vince. Neither could shed any light on his quandary, which was the absence of a theory to tie Kondratiev's waves to the sum of human behavior.

Rose, whose mind he respected, thought he was being driven by a false premise. The entire population contributed to the business cycle with supply and demand driving the activities that produced ups and downs. When the utility of expensive jewelry, designer clothes and fancy cars came into question, as an example, people with money pulled back, bought less, and forced the system to slow down in a self-correcting act. Vince, not having studied the results of Kondratiev's work, thought that major events such as wars and changes in governments (Czarism replaced by Bolshevism) were far more important forces than the aggregate of the moods of the people.

Rob knew he didn't need in any absolute sense that additional piece missing from Kondratiev's work. He really needed plenty of food in his basement. By Christmas of 2009, unemployment had gone up another percentage point. Inflation was gaining strength. Many businesses in retail were closing as were more than a few in manufacturing.

Rob heard through his children that Rose had moved to Vince's house and that his daughter Harriet had left her apartment in order to move into the family home with her husband and child. The university's pension fund put all retirees on notice that there could be a cut in the monthly distribution. Be forewarned, they were saying.

At Christmastime, Rob and Rose's son drove out. He lived in Chestnut Hill and had saved up enough gasoline for the round trip. He came with his wife bearing gifts for the season: a ham, chocolates and four bottles of red wine. The couple stayed in the guest bedroom and they feasted on the provisions they had brought, including two of the bottles of red. Rob's son was eager to find out how his father was getting along. Rob admitted to a great deal of reading and claimed he had renewed his interest in classical music. He had found a bridge partner who called himself "Grand Slam" Baker. They played as partners on alternate Tuesdays. Rob had become a steady Lutheran whose good attendance record was made possible by the Gunthers' predictable driving schedule.

Rob's son had lost his job on the newspaper while his wife still worked teaching the use of computers at the high school in her neighborhood.

The winter turned out to be mild in the mid-Atlantic region, which acted as a buttress against the doom and gloom the economic news brought. By the end of March the first signs of spring occurred. Leaf buds were on trees and there was a general awakening among the people Rob knew. That would be neighbors, bridge players, and church goers. The birds returned early.

On the last day of March, as Rob would remember it, a woman walked from the village, past the Gunther's, to his house. It was the end of the afternoon. Rob would say the sun had set. He came around the side of his house, back from inspecting the garden, when he saw her standing still and looking in his direction. The road might be forty feet away. She waved at him and he said hello and walked toward her. He saw that she had a backpack and sleeping bag strapped to her shoulders and was pulling a bag with wheels that one uses to carry clothes onto a plane. She moved a few feet toward him. She had on a wool cap and was wearing gloves. He was not certain that the weather called for them. "I stopped at your neighbors. They suggested I might come and talk to you."

"The Gunthers. Did you meet both Mary and Emil?"

"Yes, I asked them for help, a little food. They said you lived alone, could help me and wouldn't mind the intrusion. She said that if you couldn't help me to come back to their place."

Rob had heard that a few people were leaving the city and migrating to the countryside where they thought they could find food, shelter and work. This had been the first person to come down his road and reach his house, as far as he knew.

"I have spare food. Why don't you come in? You can tell me your situation."

"That's wonderfully hospitable," the lady said.

Rob took the bag with wheels and carried it up the three steps to the porch. He opened the door to let her in, followed her into the house, and put down the bag.

"I have always thought that when a moment such as this came along, the first question I'd ask was whether the person wanted to use the bathroom?"

"Yes, please. That's so nice."

"Just go up. It's at the head of the stairs."

Rob got out bread, cheese and milk and prepared an open-faced sandwich. In a few minutes she returned and he said, "Late lunch for a traveler."

She came in and sat down at the kitchen table. He said nothing as she ate half the sandwich.

"My name is Rob Doran. And yours?"

"Meg Milliken. My name is Margaret but it's always been Meg."

"And what are you doing away from home base, out in the countryside?"

"Well, Philadelphia is home base. I didn't want to continue struggling. Lost my job almost three months ago. I've never been a great saver. When the end came, that would be the end of the money, I packed a few things, gave the keys for the apartment to the doorman, emptied my bank account, came a third of the way by train and I've walked the rest of the way."

"Have you been sleeping out?"

"Yes. Not bad with a sleeping bag. It hasn't rained the last two days."

"What did your life consist of, may I ask?"

"I worked in a department store. I occupied myself with women's clothes, mostly at the high end. That market has dried up, as you can imagine."

He listened to her voice. She spoke without an accent and he guessed she had attended a college, perhaps one in the vicinity. It would all come out. He cut another slice of bread and said, "Leave space for supper. I'll fill you with vegetables and a little fruit."

"Thank you, sir," she answered.

When she had finished eating he looked out. Nightfall had come. He said to her, "Meg, you shouldn't spend nights outside. Why don't you take the guest room tonight? Get out of your hiking outfit, take a hot shower and come down for dinner."

He realized that he was inviting her to share his house but he needed the human contact. He guessed that she would pull her weight around the place, or hoped she would. He carried her bag up to the guest bedroom. "There are towels in the bathroom closet," he said.

"You don't know how wonderful running hot water is until you haven't had any for a couple of days," she said.

He went downstairs and thought about dinner. He did have limited choice but he would open a bottle of red wine, the last of the four his son and daughter-in-law had brought out at Christmas. Vegetables, cheese, bread and stewed fruit would have to do. He heard the shower running for a bit longer than he used it but he knew women washed their hair and rinsed it. Perhaps twenty minutes had elapsed before she came down. He was surprised at the outfit. Her hair was still wet, but combed straight out. She wore a green polypropylene shirt that hikers wear. These shirts are designed to hug the body. They have full length sleeves. The purpose of being tight on the body was to bring the moisture off the skin to the other side so that it could evaporate and keep the athlete dry. The green shirt hugged Meg and accentuated her breasts. Rob guessed that she had studied herself in the mirror a few times with the shirt on and hoped that the occasion would arise when she could wear it as part of an outfit, all by itself. As she walked across the kitchen, her breasts moved inside her shirt. Her nipples appeared to be partially erect. Rob thought he knew what the sleeping arrangement would be that night. The remainder of her clothes consisted of a full skirt, green woolen stockings, and a pair of loafers.

She came to the stove and asked how she might help. He said that dinner was ready to go on the table. He poured two glasses of wine and then they started talking. She had no family in Philadelphia. Her mother's people were centered in Pittsburgh and her father's in Toledo. There was a lone brother who lived in Pittsburgh and while she could have gone to either city and the relatives there would have taken her in, she believed she would be a burden. She explained that they were not rich and did not live in large houses. "What I'm doing now, roughing it, moving around on my own, that's so much more sensible." She paused for a moment then added, "I have to be responsible. I'm almost fifty." That's how she summed up her position. Then she added, "I still have eighteen dollars in my purse."

They talked during dinner, mostly about his life and how he had come to be living on his own place in the country. He reviewed his career and told her that he had retired a year or so previously, and that his wife was still in the city.

They discussed the financial crisis and how both of them were becoming accustomed to it. It no longer seemed to be a crisis now that more than two years of it had gone by. Meg referred to it as a condition, which would last as long as it had to and would go away when it was ready to move on.

They cleared the table, and washed and dried the dishes. They left the important discussions for tomorrow. Would she want to stay? Would he want her to stay? "Bedtime comes early for me," he said.

"Shall I use the bathroom first?" she asked.

"Good idea," he answered.

"I'll leave my door ajar," she said.

WAVES IN OUR LIVES
PART 7

They had finished a simple breakfast of hot cereal and coffee. It might have been eight o'clock. The radio was on with the news. "What's your take on last night, Meg?"

"The end of a wonderful day. I was tired of walking, had been turned down a few times. It was getting dark and I found you and your warm hospitality. Can you imagine how I felt? The shower and dinner. Then late last night. You're a sweet, soft lover. It's been almost three years since the previous man and I was so pleased to be with you."

"I suppose it's been a year since I left my wife. Do you think we could make a go of it? I have to guess that you want to live in the country."

"We can give it a try. I'm a good worker and have a green thumb developed as a youngster. The challenge is to see how we fit in emotionally."

"Maybe it would grow into love," Rob said.

"Wouldn't that be idyllic?" Meg answered. "By the way, what's the building out back? I can see it from the bathroom window."

"The creation of a previous owner. He must have wanted more than a tool shed and less than a second home. I've always imagined that he and his wife needed distance between them, perhaps fifty feet. We ought to measure it."

"I could see wires going out to the building. Does it have water as well?" Meg asked.

"Yes, and gas. My guess is that it was built as a tool shed and a place to repair farm implements. I can see the previous gentleman sharpening knives, placing a new handle on an axe, and perhaps cleaning and fixing a carburetor."

"Can we look inside?"

"We go there to get gardening tools, so, yes, we'll go inside."

It was a clear, warm day and they did not don extra clothing. "Are we taking out tools for work?" Meg asked.

"On second thought, why don't we just look in? I thought we would walk around, show you the place and pick up a few branches for the fireplace tonight."

When they returned to it, Meg examined the tool house with care. She noted that there was a toilet and a sink but no shower, and that while a bathroom of sorts existed there was no roughed-out kitchen. She remarked on this and Rob asked her why she was so interested in the livability of the building.

"Plenty of other people will follow me out of the city and they'll want to occupy this space."

They went over the work required to finish the building to make it habitable. There would need to be a shower and the makings of a kitchen along with the addition of a potbelly stove to burn wood and heat the space. The building was twenty-by-thirty feet and had two floors. The second floor could be converted into a bedroom but the ceiling would need to be insulated. The project would not be impossible but would take time and money. Rob could see that Meg would be interested in the project and that changing a shell into a home appealed to her more than gardening.

In spite of the distraction of the second building, Meg turned out to be a competent, willing gardener. She indeed had learned a fair amount from her mother and threw herself into preparing the soil and planting the crops they would harvest and can as these crops turned into vegetables. Meg suggested that they should buy fruit locally, particularly peaches and apples and "put them up," as she expressed it. She calculated their needs for a year and added twenty-five percent over that amount. "You can never tell who might show up," she explained.

Their days fell into a regular pattern soon enough: work outdoors in the morning; lunch and a nap, followed frequently by love-making; gathering wood and cutting it to length in the afternoon; preparing and having dinner, followed by reading.

They had never stopped sleeping together in the guestroom. The main bedroom was larger and had more attractive furniture than Meg's room did, although the beds were identical. After Meg had been in the house for two weeks, Rob suggested that she install herself in the main bedroom. "It's more comfortable, a bit less cramped. The move does symbolize that you are the lady of the house and I have to tell you that I'm feeling the first twinges of love."

"You are a warm and affectionate man and I'm certain you loved your wife for those forty years."

"True, but at the end I couldn't muster total, absolute love because it turned out that the combination of wanting to live in the country and believing that civilization was grinding to a halt made me give her up. So I did not have infinite love for Rose. How about you?"

"The two men I lived with, I loved them both. We fell apart over having children. I wanted to marry and have two kids but neither could satisfy that need in me. It was a damned shame because they were good men except for that failing."

"Well, a major failing, as you suggest."

"Love's coming in me for you slowly. It's too late for children. You're a sweet, uncomplicated man and there's nothing this woman wants to change in you. We certainly lead a simple life and I hadn't realized that the irritations of city life can get in the way of the flow of affection back and forth."

"You mention that you can no longer have children. It's another miracle of nature that in the early years you can reproduce but when that's over, the pleasures of sex remain for quite a few years. A very generous move on the part of the creator."

"Yes. It's starting to restore belief in me. I'm glad I'm attending services with you and the real Lutherans next door. I consider you a recently forged Lutheran."

Their conversations were frequently an analysis of the news that they had heard on the radio. Television programming had become spotty with the result that they did not turn on their set. They discussed the books they read, doing their best to read the same books. It seemed natural to read the classics of English and American literature and to read the important translations from other languages. Meg enjoyed what they were doing but stayed with *War and Peace* when Rob elected to read Plutarch. They arranged their reading schedules to finish books at approximately the same time, for purposes of lengthy discussions. Meg would stay home when Rob went out to play bridge, the occasion being reduced to once per month. Meg refused to learn the game.

"Games provide you with a bit of pleasure but there is so little residue," she would say.

Meg was more interested than Rob in the situation around her. She wanted to find the stores, see what they had in stock, what the prices were and how much they had gone up. She also was interested in selling a bit of their surplus food, only to find out that others in the county were selling theirs.

One day, apropos of nothing, Rob told Meg that his wife owned half the property. "You've been thinking about it?" she asked.

"Yes. It's been on my mind to tell you. The inheritance from my father was specific, that the money could be used for the pleasure of both parties and then he named them, 'my son Robinson and his wife Rose.'"

"She could show up with a surveyor, cut the property in half and sell off her portion," Meg said. "When Rose did not object to the purchase at the time, I thought she was sanctioning the idea of my buying it," Rob said. "In any event, you should not be surprised if that long-dormant volcano comes to life one of these days."

On matters religious, Meg had joined Rob and the Gunthers for church on Sundays. They never missed. Meg was attracted to the women who participated in any event that brought them together. Sewing quilts was number one on her list because the women at the church worked on these quilts as a group, not individually. Meg did not see a faster way of getting to know people in the area and in picking up the news. Rob called it gossip but Meg insisted that it was news. Among the women working on them, a few did keep quilts for themselves, but the principal purpose was to sell them at fairs and from small stores. A woman who elected to keep a quilt that she had worked on with others would give up receiving the proceeds from the sale of other quilts. These were some of the few products that could command a price when offered to the public.

Rob determined that Meg's interest in making The Shack habitable had as much to do with her interests in crafts than in anything else. She said to Rob one day that they ought to start on either the kitchen or the bathroom, adding a stove and a sink in the kitchen and a shower in the bathroom. Then they needed a hot water heater. The public utility that provided the electricity also piped natural gas to the area. The electricity had come in during the New Deal as part of rural electrification. Gas had followed soon after. Most customers used a small amount of both, being unwilling to cancel service on one for fear that the other might suspend delivery, for any number of reasons.

Meg threw herself into the project of making the kitchen and bathroom serviceable. "You're moving out, is that it?" Rob asked her one day.

"No. The news from the cities isn't positive and we may be having guests," Meg answered.

"Could these be former associates of yours?" he asked.

"You never know. One more food riot like last week's could put plenty of people on the road. Philadelphia emptying out. Be prepared, that's what I say."

When the growing and canning season had ended, Meg put Rob to work finishing the project. They found used appliances and rented a truck to move them to the property. Emil Gunther was recruited to connect these new appliances and test them. A man of a few words, he pronounced the job done to his satisfaction by saying, "Everything seems to work." Rob and Meg gave him a case of the beer he drank. He had refused money.

WAVES in our LIVES
PART 8

Although Rob had been in the countryside a year longer than Meg had, they both felt, on examination, that the flexible, resourceful parts of human beings were at work in them, changing them sufficiently to accommodate their new status. In addition, they were in love and pleased at this outcome. "The professor and the dress designer," she would say of themselves, although she did not design clothes, only selected what would be for sale in her section of the department store.

Rob was not able to suppress his need to talk about Kondratiev. It came under the title of unfinished business. He explained to Meg the concept of the business cycle, which she had no difficulty grasping. "Anyone not understanding the ups and downs in the economy would be living on Mars." She reworded the statement to, "Anyone who did not know there were ups and downs in the economy would be living on Mars."

Rob went on to explain that Kondratiev had not produced a theory for the existence of waves, approximately fifty to sixty years in duration. He did suggest that savings were required to make capital available for the production of goods in the event demand for them surfaced, but he published no grand theory on the existence of his waves. Rob told Meg that he wanted to connect the variations in the economic cycle to mood swings in the public.

Meg responded immediately saying that the public had to be divided into segments appropriately before any general theory could be formulated. "Tell me about those mortgages. I suppose they are at the bottom of our troubles." Before starting in on mortgages, Rob said, "For mortgages to bring down the system, to the extent that they have, the system had to be frail and ready to have a correction at the least provocation." "Fair enough," Meg said.

"Well, I'll keep it simple. You're a bank and you find one thousand customers from all your branches who wish to buy a house. The bank creates one thousand mortgages for them as customers buy houses. The bank bundles these mortgages and sells them to an insurance company, or an agency of the federal government, or, as the originator, the bank keeps the mortgages until they're all paid off."

"That's what I'd do, take the third choice," Meg commented. "That stream of gold coming in each month. Love it."

Rob continued. "I don't know the formula but the bankers suspected they could make more money by selling the mortgages. They then have the money back to lend once again. Do you want to know how they got into trouble?"

"May as well tell me. It's raining this afternoon anyway."

"Well, here's an example. It's not the only step to take to get into trouble but it was one of them. Let's say you take the one thousand mortgages and put them into three equal stacks, A, B and C. The mortgages are not selected in any way; they just land in one of the three piles. The bank sells the mortgages in pile A to an investor, telling this investor that he will have first crack at the revenue coming in from those customers paying on the one thousand mortgages. If only a third of households make their payments then the owner of A gets all the money. The owner of pile A gets 5% interest per year and pays a premium for his three hundred and thirty-three mortgages. The investor buying pile B gets 6% interest as his annual return and is next in line for the mortgage payments. He pays no premium. The investor buying pile C gets 7% interest annually and is last in line for a monthly payment, and he buys pile C at a discount. If a third of homeowners default, then this investor receives nothing for that month."

"When a few homeowners default, the investor who bought C sure gets shortchanged," Meg said.

"And the bank has a non-performing loan that must be marked to market. So the bank takes a house valued at $300,000 and marks it down to $150,000, say, guided by a similar drop in price in the area. The bank assumes it could seize the property and auction it off at that price. I'm making up these numbers to illustrate a point."

"I figured you were doing that. Are there more gory parts to the story?"

"Yes, there are other ways of slicing and selling off mortgages but suffice to say that the financial people were inventive, all in the name of earning another commission or fee. But let me switch to the insurance part of the story, and then I'll stop. The investors who bought A or B or C imagined that they could lose their investment. It turned out that plenty of homeowners walked away from their homes and left the keys in the mailbox.

The logical thing to do is to insure the asset. So the investors go to an insurance company, which calculates the premium, and the insurance company draws up an insurance policy that the investors start to pay on. When a number of homeowners stop paying on their mortgages, then a default exists and the insurance company must make the owners of the policy whole, if the insurance company has enough money in the till."

"That's bad stuff," Meg said.

"I'll tell you one more detail and then stop. Is that OK?"

"I can take it as long as I'm learning."

"The final piece is that speculators, sensing an opportunity, go to the insurance company and buy the same policy, even though they do not have a mortgage, and they own no part of A, B or C. They just want to play poker, get a piece of the action, I think it's called," Rob said. "The insurance company says, why not? Business is business, but of course risks mount for the insurance company in the event the housing industry collapsed, which it did."

"Plenty of hanky-panky going on. You can stop there, Rob."

"Well, that's the gist of it. Nothing that I described is against the law. It just represents poor business practices. Creating all those damaged assets cost the taxpayers billions because the government didn't want the financial markets and banks to fail."

"What would you have done?" Meg asked.

"That's different from what I would have been able to do. I would have chained a leg of each important executive to a leg of his/her desk and let them work on solutions for the problems they created."

"Lunch and bathroom breaks?"

"Yes, and they even could go home at night, but they couldn't waltz off to retirement or to another job. The geniuses that created the mess know more of the details than anyone else in the country. Let them stew in their juices and undo the harm, or try to undo the harm."

"We were talking about old Kondtratiev and his waves," Meg said. "How did we get off on this tangent?"

"I want to tie the business cycle into the psychological trends in the population and I thought you needed examples in order to evaluate my thoughts."

"Well, all the charlatans came for lunch. Surely someone who buys a house with no plan to pay for it is a rascal, and the persons that made it possible, the lenders, they're rascals as well, aiders, abettors, cheerleaders. They make their money and manage to step out of the way just before the ladder falls or the dam bursts," Meg said.

"So, to construct my theory, we need a segment of the population we'll call rascals. Is that it?" Rob asked.

"Yes, but let me add that these rascals exist at all times in the society. A situation such as you describe just allows rascals to show their faces. It gives them an opportunity to practice all the chicanery lying about in their personalities."

"The trait is there all the time," Rob said. "Making the tie-in is a complex matter. That may be why Kondratiev didn't touch it."

"I'm going to take the plunge, Rob, and just say that the business cycle and human nature are connected at the hip. Events bring to the fore persons with particular personality traits and these individuals can cause ripples in the business cycle. I'm leaving it to you to sort it out."

Before Rob could speak, Meg interjected, "No, wait a minute. The population needs to be segmented, and segmented in different ways at different times in the business cycle. When bad times come, rich people may stop buying fancy dresses from me but if they're scheduled to buy a new car every third year they won't upset that plan. And on mortgages, the home owners who already have a mortgage to go with their house, they may not play a part in the disaster we've seen. And the banks going to the brink of extinction; that has nothing to do with depositors and everything to do with the senior managers at banks who lost their bearings. So you need to break down the population into the proper segments and assign responsibility where it belongs."

"You're certain you were an English major?" Rob asked.

"Had I had more energy I would have taken a language seriously, such as Russian or French. But I realized I could earn a degree while spending a good part of four years reading those great authors. What a bargain!"

Rob knew he should take Meg seriously. Not one of his friends or acquaintances had advanced the notion she had with such brevity. He would get out paper and pencil and see what he could diagram. There was little doubt that Meg had a fertile mind and would come up with other suggestions. He wanted to tell her that she had wasted her talents by busying herself with the fancy gowns for the women of Philadelphia, but thought better of it.

As he went over what she had said, Rob realized that her solution was too complicated. All the great theories that describe the workings of the universe were simple, just a few letters on each side of an equal sign. Newton's classic, $F = MA$, came to his mind: force equals mass times acceleration. He might be able to work her thoughts into his general theory, but he couldn't segregate the population into various groups, each acting according to a particular stimulus. He would require of himself additional work that might bring on the final insight.

WAVES IN OUR LIVES
PART 9

M eg and Rob were settling in for what they called the long haul. Even though times were hard they had reached a steady state. Unemployment was holding at twelve percent and inflation had abated. This didn't mean prices were going down, just that they weren't going up anymore. They held at their peak and Rob surmised that there was insufficient demand for many commodities and products to drive prices upwards.

There were areas of the California and Arizona deserts that held jet liners, awaiting an upturn in air traffic. Acres and acres of fully operational planes soaking up the desert sun, waiting to fly again. The airlines that had parked their planes covered their identifying marks with a thick cover of white paint.

The amount of money sitting there, lying idle, was not beyond calculation but those who drove by had no stomach for multiplying the number of planes in view by sixty million dollars, an average value. Airlines over the world replaced their own aging fleets with the best picks among the parked planes. The two major manufacturers of commercial jets shared what little business that remained, much of it refurbishing planes they had rolled out new ten to fifteen years earlier.

Train traffic picked up because the all-electric locomotives consumed power generated in nuclear plants. It was recognized that using electricity generated in a nuclear power plant was about as free of carbon dioxide as possible. The only carbon dioxide generated came out of the lungs of the workers. High speed electric trains were installed between major centers, with the result that a great number of cars left the highways. Airlines were allowed to merge with railroad companies and either could run a fleet of trucks or merge with a trucking company, so that anyone needing to move freight could select the least expensive solution, in many cases using two out of the three methods. The use of corporate jets retuned when class warfare was put aside and voters across the nation admitted that the time saved by executives was of great value. One executive was quoted as saying, "Time is all I have."[2]

Meg felt that the slow pace that had been adopted as normal around the country was a healthy step. "People are reading more and running around less," she said. Her routine included four hours of work, six days per week. She gardened, cooked, canned vegetables and fruit, and kept both places ship-shape. Rob gardened with Meg, took charge of his forest, and built a pond by damning a natural declivity and having their stream fill it. He bought a gasoline-driven pump which could be used to fight a fire, either in one of the buildings or outdoors.

They both looked fit and trim, and accommodated to their existence by dressing as casually as one could. They walked together to the general store to check the mail box. If it was not convenient they would miss a day and, as Meg said, "We only miss the gossip. There's rarely any mail."

---

[2]   Direct quote from Winston S. Churchill

The maternity wards in hospitals were less busy than they had been for decades. Pediatricians were concentrating on fly-fishing. The phenomenon of a lower birthrate was on everyone's lips. The consensus held that children were too expensive to raise, and when the time came their neighborhood schools might be closed. Because entertainment of high quality was difficult to come by, sex lives improved in quality and frequency while cheating on one's spouse diminished considerably. There were fewer business trips, fewer late afternoon trysts, and fewer people willing to risk all for a few moments of pleasure.

Those individuals holding jobs eliminated the forty-hour work week and substituted one lasting thirty hours. Eight to five with an hour for lunch gave way to nine to five with coffee breaks and longer lunches to bring time at work to about six hours per day, or thirty hours per week. The concept of keeping stores open on Sunday vanished as there wasn't enough purchasing power around to provide shoppers with the necessary where-with-all.

Public education took an interesting turn. Students now wished to consider themselves cultured more than anything else. English became the favorite course and the ability to express one's self appropriately was prized. As a result there appeared a strong demand for teachers of English, Latin, Greek and the modern European languages. Knowing Latin gave students the ability on some occasions to say "verdant umbrage" in place of "green shade," using words that had originated with Latin instead of German. Besides an acquaintance with Latin and Greek, students expected of themselves to be fluent in a modern language, such as German or Spanish.

History and geography became popular on the basis that persons should know a great deal about the planet they lived on. General knowledge replaced general ignorance, which had been the norm for so many years. Mathematics and the hard sciences were studied because they were difficult to master and led frequently to jobs that paid money. Students dreaded the search for a job after high school or after college and for that reason worked hard during their young years.

Many people of all ages returned to the country and bragged that their grandparents or great-grandparents had worked on a farm, or perhaps grown up on one. The attraction of farm life was the availability of food. Ten people from several generations might operate a twenty-acre farm with no difficulty. There would be chickens, cows and pigs to provide the necessities. Corn would be grown to make silage for the animals to eat, and the usual potatoes, vegetables and fruits were planted, gown, harvested and preserved. The planting of corn to make ethanol was discontinued when it was recognized that corn was a food meant for consumption by two-and four-legged animals. Furthermore, one got more miles in a car from a gallon of gasoline than from a gallon of ethanol.

Most countries decided to reduce the size of their military forces on the basis that they were too expensive. The people that made up the military establishment could design extraordinary weapons that would do the job better than the previous generation of weapons but they became too expensive to manufacture. Most countries were forced to lose interest in all but the rudimentary weapons.

Governments became conscious of budgetary limitations. The small towns were well run because the populace was close to their government. The larger towns and counties were forced to emphasize maintenance over new projects. States and the federal government were the last entities to get religion and trim expenses.

In order to promote the payment of taxes, the tax codes in various jurisdictions around the country were simplified, a needed reform as incomes fell. The federal government kept the old tax code with its 20,000 pages of regulations but the Congress instituted an alternate code with twenty lines, which in effect swept away the old code. The new code was called an income tax because it taxed income at reduced rates and got rid of all the appendages.

Americans still traveled on vacations. Small trailers were towed behind the family car. A configuration of canvas and metal rods that became a tent was carried in the trailer along with food, clothes and a stove. Camping increased in popularity. Motels cut their rates and looked the other way when children slept in the car and used the shower. Dishes and pots were washed in the bathroom sink and cooking outdoors was permitted. Parents still wanted their children to see the United States. The three-week trips to Europe became the exception.

One night, Meg said, "Sweetheart, I have you." Rob reflected for a moment and said, "You came down the road as I was returning from the woods. Had I been a minute earlier or later I would have missed you. What a gift you've been." He paused and added, "You woke up so much desire in me with that skin-tight green shirt of yours.'

"It worked as planned. It had the desired effect."

"Still does," he said

They were very close, Rob thought. Same values, same aims in life, he reasoned. He enjoyed her sweet, natural and warm temperament. Rob thought she knew all there was to know about the love act.

It was a Saturday evening in April of 2012 when Vince telephoned.

WAVES IN OUR LIVES
PART 10

"Well, this is a surprise, Vince. To what do I owe this?"
"Your dear wife is hankering for a drive to the country to visit you, the new lady in your life, and measure the changes in you, from professor to farmer."

"Just pick a time and drive on out. We attend services Sunday morning, a new adventure for me, but any other day of the week is fine. You can plan to stay overnight in the little house."

Vince signed off, promising to call back in a day or two. On having been alerted, Meg went directly to the reason. "She wants you back; it couldn't be anything else. Can't tell whether she wants to be here with you or have you back in the city."

"She's a fine person, as you will see," Rob said. "But I'm so pleased to be with you. I really don't look forward to any change." They were silent and then Rob added, "We could contemplate living in the city when this long, painful episode with the economy is over, but that would be to accommodate a need on your part to resume your career. I'm perfectly happy with our life in the country."

They were at the kitchen sink. Rob let the water run cold and drank a half glass. "My wife may want a divorce in which case we could marry although I would be navigating through uncharted waters, an old wreck moving along without a plan."

"You're a sweet old wreck and thanks for the hint of marriage, but you can't leave this life before you finish with Kondratiev."

"Right you are, Meg. I have to write that paper before the people I know at the financial journals all retire."

Vince held to his promise and telephoned in a couple of days. "We'll take you up on your offer. Come out on Wednesday and stay overnight. Get the full experience. Can we bring anything?"

"We have plenty of food in the basement but we're always short on red wine, scotch and bourbon." "I'll bring a bar for us," Vince said.

"So it was not Rose, but Vince again. I wonder why she would decide against talking to you directly," Meg said.

"Probably that the conversation would wander off into the topics she wants to bring up to me, saving all that for face-to-face," Rob speculated.

The first telephone call had been on Saturday. Vince's confirming call came on Monday. They arrived on Wednesday after lunch. Meg dressed for the moment in jeans with a crease ironed in and a white blouse reasonably tight across the front. There was a small scarf around her neck to add color. She had put on lipstick.

They walked out to greet the visitors. Rose wore a cotton dress. She did not allow trousers in her social wardrobe. Her hair was shorter than Rob remembered it.

"Two good looking women," Rob thought as he made introductions. Rose and Vince left their overnight bags in the car when the four of them moved into the house. There were flattering remarks passed around. Meg offered tea, which they all accepted.

"Just as I remember it," Rose said about the larger house when she returned with Meg from looking at the upstairs. Meg hadn't made any changes except to put out photographs of her family, which were sent to her by various members. Rose asked about them and then wanted to know if Meg was happy in the country. "I know you used to work and live downtown," Rose said.

"I'm surprised that it suits me so well. I moved out when I ran out of money. Rob took me in, a great piece of luck for me."

When the four were downstairs and tea finished, Meg said to Vince, "Let me show you the grounds. We can take your bags out of the car and leave them in the other place."

They were off, leaving Rob and Rose alone. There were a few preliminary remarks between them. Rose watched Meg and Vince walk to the smaller house. When they came out of the house and turned to the woods, Rose looked at Rob and said, "We're still married and I'd love to have you back."

"I recall clearly that you told me that if I moved out to the country I could consider the marriage over, no matter what the documents said."

"That was then. This is now," Rose said.

"My arrangement is stable. I like Meg. I could extend that and say that I love her," Rob said.

"I've had three years with Vince. He's fine but after forty years with you I'm spoiled. He's not the same high quality that you got me accustomed to. Remember, it was you who decided to leave me."

Rob did not allow himself to react. "Is Vince happy?" he asked.

"Yes, I would say close to delirious. He can't get quite enough of me. I could be bragging."

"No, you're not bragging. He's always been high on you," Rob said.

"Are you and Meg simpatico?" Rose asked. "She's more of an armful than I imagined."

"Well, yes, it works out very well between us," Rob said.

"If you change your mind, let me know. I have the inheritance from my aunt and we could buy a house. Houses are not expensive now."

"What would I do with Meg?" Rob asked.

"You could give her to Vince. He might not notice."

"I think Meg would," Rob said. He knew the exchange had run into the ground and changed the topic. They discussed events in their former neighborhood, what had happened to some of their close friends, and how their children were getting along.

Meg and Vince returned and Vince noted that it was cocktail hour. They moved two additional chairs to the porch and made their favorites. "I'm taking this basket back to Philadelphia empty," Vince said. "If you drink less tonight there will be more for the future," Vince added.

"Good now, good later," Rob said.

They had dinner featuring vegetables from the basement. Rob had bought beef as a supplement. He and Meg tended to have meat once a week. The conversation was not strained nor was it strong. They could not settle on a theme and explore it to a conclusion. They broke up early and were in bed before ten.

"How did it go with Rose and you?" Meg asked.

"She wants a reconciliation, which I turned down. I told her that you and I were settled and happy."

"And what did she say to that?"

"She left it open. I might have added that it was a closed matter with you and me, but I thought that was obvious."

"My guess is that they will be off before ten in the morning."

On that note they moved upstairs to prepare for bed.

When they had finished breakfast, Rose and Vince returned to the smaller house to pack. As Meg had guessed they were off by ten. Meg and Rob changed into gardening clothes and sallied forth for a morning of planting and weeding. They stayed together in the early afternoon when they walked in the woods in search for fallen branches for a fire that evening. They always found dead branches for kindling while many logs came all at once when Rob chopped or sawed a dead tree.

The arrival of Rose and her suggestion that Rob come back to her had destabilizing effects. There was no doubt that Rob and Meg were evaluating the offer, each in their own way. Meg would be thinking that Rob was reviewing the positive aspects of returning to the city and picking up where he left off with Rose. Rob guessed that city life, or at least the promise of it, would be moving through Meg's mind. She would be thinking about the pleasures of reviving her career and renewing the friendships left behind.

Rob let a week go by before he felt that it would be natural to love Meg once again. They had never gone this long. It was the shadow of Rose in bed with them that caused the damage. Rob was upset that Rose could sleep with Vince and suggest a change in partners so easily, as though emotional attachment could be engaged and disengaged with the snap of a finger. It was another week before the impact of Rose diminished sufficiently for Rob and Meg that they could reconstitute the lives of two people in love.

The balance of the year 2012 and the start of 2013 gave no evidence of abatement to the dismal economic conditions. Millions of Americans were becoming accustomed to a lower standard of living than they had known in the previous decade. All manner of shortcuts were invented to maintain an agreeable life style without including luxuries. Many people reflected that while their standard of living had diminished—less money to spend—their quality of life had gone up as they had more time for meaningful activities. Things meant less; people meant more.

In the year that spanned the spring of 2012 to the same time in 2013, Meg and Rob carried on, gradually expanding their horizons. There were more trips to Lancaster, a weekend in Philadelphia, and talk of spending a few days in Atlantic City. They were not interested in gambling but longed for time in the ocean. "I need to see you in a bathing suit," Rob had said. "I can buy a suit and wear it around the house," Meg answered.

On the weekend they were in Philadelphia, they drove to Meg's last address. The same doorman was still employed. "What ever happened to my furniture?" Meg asked him after going through formalities. "We packed up your things and put them in the basement. Do you want to see your place? No one's rented it."

Meg was not particularly interested but Rob was curious about her previous life. They took the elevator to the fourth floor. After a tour of the rooms, Rob wanted to know which landmarks of the city he could spot from the living room window.

In the spring of 2013, Meg received a letter from her former supervisor at the department store. It was written by hand. Meg read out loud the woman's name from the return address on the back of the envelope. Meg and she had written and talked on the phone intermittently. Rob knew that Meg and she had a close, personal relationship.

WAVES IN OUR LIVES
PART 11

M eg did not open the envelope in the post office, realizing that she would be expected to make a remark to Rob, which would be overheard by the lady postmaster.

When they were outside the store Meg said, "It's from Alexis. Dear, funny, woman. If you are intended to have a boss, she's the best type." Meg read the letter to Rob as they walked along. It contained an invitation to come to Philadelphia and visit her at the store. To be negotiated were the terms under which Meg could return to work. The rich people of Philadelphia were starting to buy clothes once again. She quoted from the letter, "The old clients are starting to spend again."

"If you went back, that would be an extraordinary change of life for both of us," Rob said.

"Of course it would be. If I go back, you are invited to come with me and share life as we have been doing."

"A change has been in the back of your mind recently, or all along?"

"I suppose a year ago I started to sense an urge to return to the city, work, earn a salary once again, you know all that stuff," Meg said.

"That touches on the fundamentals. We are not supposed to live out our lives in the countryside if we are city people at heart. Do you think that explains it?" Rob asked

"Some people such as our dear neighbors the Gunthers and Stewards are at home in their places and situations. I don't think any of the four of them wants to go back where they came from. For myself I have to admit that I miss the pace and the contacts. Here all my stimulation must come from you. I must say you are a terrific stimulant," Meg said.

"That's very generous. I love stimulating you," Rob answered.

"I know you do. I was about to add that in the city I'm in regular contact with more and different people, and there are all the cultural events. I have to tell you that I've missed that and in the last year I've missed it a great deal."

"What do you plan to do about the letter?" Rob asked.

"I'll telephone tomorrow and we'll set up something."

"Will you want me to drive you in?"

"No need. Just take me to the train station. We'll look at the schedule and decide which train I'm taking back."

Meg's friend and former supervisor was named Alexis Peters. She and Meg were a fine fit. Alexis enjoyed managing affairs and people while Meg's interests centered on keeping up with fashion and dressing women properly for all occasions. Meg telephoned Alexis that afternoon and they made an appointment for the day following.

"Plan to spend mid-day here. We'll factor in lunch. I'll be expecting you," Alexis said.

Rob could not hide his disappointment. "I have, we have, a complete life here. We have one another. We're busy. There's plenty of reward in accomplishing a modicum of self-sufficiency. I think the love between us is strong. Are you certain you want to give up all that?"

"No, not certain. A minute ago I told you what I miss about city life. Perhaps I didn't emphasize the appeal of restarting my career. That I miss, really. And what would happen if you came and we lived together? We could get to know one another's friends from before."

"It might work," Rob admitted. "I'd have to find a new set of occupations to interest me. Right now, planting, weeding and managing my ten acres seems to fill the time adequately. Back in the city I'd have to start over."

"That's true. You didn't experience retirement in the city. You finished at the university and came to the country in one motion. So you don't have activities to return to."

They had made it through the evening. Rob took her in his arms as he did every night. He told her that he loved her, again which he told her every night. He told her that she had to do what was best for her and that if she returned to the city, he might not come along. They embraced and kissed and that was the extent of it. They were mostly silent in the morning, knowing that while it might be an exciting day for Meg it would be painfully slow for Rob.

Alexis was standing at the door of her office. They hugged, told one another how well the other looked, and in a few sentences celebrated the partial return of good times. Alexis told Meg that at the start of the downturn any evidence of ostentation was kept in check. Alexis speculated that it was the men in the family who put on the brakes. She told Meg about a woman whose daughter was coming out. Mother and daughter flew to Chicago and went through the wardrobes of this woman's sister and daughter to select dresses for the party in Philadelphia. "The important thing is to wear something that no one's seen before."

When times had ceased getting worse, people with money felt that they could spend some of it without causing a furor. "As I understand it," Alexis explained, "the rich, most of them, always have money. It starts with the grandfather, passes on to the father, then to the son. These people do not wish to let on about their situation beyond what they can't help showing. They can't hide the house, the cars, country club membership, club membership downtown and a fine life style. They can hide ostentatious behavior. They own apartment buildings, office buildings, parking lots and pieces of small banks in their part of town. They get good educations. Careful parents insist on it." Meg interrupted to say, "The women manage to get their hands on enough money. Their men seem not to begrudge it."

They went on to discuss how it became fashionable to spend less but there were occasions that called for splurging, such as a fiftieth birthday party when rules were set aside.

On the matter of salary, Alexis suggested that Meg start at her previous level adjusted upwards by eighty percent to compensate for inflation. A few minutes before noon, Alexis announced that Meg would be having lunch with the store manager, who had come from headquarters six months previously. "He wants to speak to new hires personally. He's about your age. Quite personable."

"Married, divorced, single, what would you guess?"

"His personnel file indicates that he's single and I've heard it whispered about that he's never been married."

"Must be something wrong with him," Meg said.

"Name's Scott Nichols," Alexis finished.

Meg had gathered a few outfits, mostly used ones for her appearances at church. She frequented second-hand stores where she could pick out clothes that did not show signs of much wear and looked well on her. She was taller than average and thought of herself as a big, slender woman. For this occasion she wore dark blue shoes with two inch heels, black silk stockings that came up to the knee, a navy blue pleated skirt that came sufficiently below the knee to hide the top of the stockings, and the white blouse she had worn when Vince and Rose had driven out. There was a purple silk scarf that she thought complemented the color of her eyes, although she admitted to herself that others might not detect a mauve shade on her.

Meg walked up one flight of stairs to Scott Nichols' office. A secretary whom she remembered announced her. As she walked in, he was putting down the telephone. He came around the desk to shake her hand. "How do you do? Things are beginning to look up," he said.

"Yes. The old customers coming back a handful at a time," Meg answered.

"It's noon and I thought we could have lunch and do our talking there. If you return to us, we'll both be employees and we might not be able to socialize this way."

"We could have business lunches," Meg volunteered. Scott made a face and said that others would be accompanying them.

Meg knew that there was a segment of the male population who went crazy over her. She was bigger than most women. She felt that the average woman would be five feet five or six, and perhaps weighed one hundred and twenty-five pounds while she was the next larger size at five feet eight and one hundred forty pounds. Rob had been taken by her. He told her soon after she moved into his house that she had awakened something in him. When she met Rose she understood that the reason could be that Rose was smaller than she and had never ignited Rob's sexual drive the way she had. Rob had been gentle but insistent. She would always remember their first nights together when he appeared to be insatiable.

The fact that Scott was talking about restrictions on employees socializing could only mean that he was attracted by her appearance. Having known one another for only a few minutes, there had not been enough time together for him to warm to her personality. If she returned to work she thought they would embark on a season of romance that would take them to an unknown destination, perhaps where they both wanted to go.

The restaurant he had selected was not far from the store. They were seated at a table with a view. The table was set with a white table cloth. This was city life.

WAVES IN OUR LIVES
PART 12

They retraced her years with the store. Scott was apologetic about management having let her go. "We can't hold you responsible for this prolonged recession, Scott," Meg said.

"Thank you for that. It's always a difficult task to let anyone go, even for unavoidable reasons."

"Tell me the signs you see about an upturn," Meg said.

"Alexis tells me that customers she hasn't seen for a couple of years have come back and those that did keep coming are coming more frequently. And their daughters, some married, some married and working, are starting to surface. I don't think Alexis is inventing any of this, even though she's eager to get off the floor and spend full time running her department."

"Here's what I added to customer relations that Alexis did not. There's not enough time for one person to do everything. She's a wonderful administrator but I don't think her heart is in dressing each customer with the clothes that suit her. The women I serve are individuals. I know their tastes; I think I know their colors and the clothes for them. As part of it, Alexis and the manager you succeeded had me take trips to New York, Paris and Milan."

"It's an enormous industry to cover well," Scott said. "Alexis tells me that you always paid for your trips with the additional sales you generated."

"Yes. When you pick out something for a particular woman, she might be the only woman in Philadelphia to wear that item. You've made a friend. And on their trips to Europe I provide them with stores to visit, along with a name of someone to talk to about clothes."

"Alexis tells me you have never married," Scott said. "Did work keep you away from it?"

"No. Men with their heels dug in kept me away from the altar. I wanted two children, a boy and a girl, of course, but that was not to be."

"For me it's been a matter of transfers to various cities and meeting the correct woman at the wrong time. I feel as though my life is a series of near misses."

"And how old are you?" she asked.

"Fifty-two and not much to show for it."

"Don't be hard on yourself, Scott. You've done well in business."

He slid his hand across the table and placed it on hers. "You're open and warm, Meg." He took his hand away and asked, "When will I know if you're coming back?"

"Tomorrow," she said.

As they walked back to the store, Meg turned to Scott and asked, "How about the remainder of the store? Do you sense that it's coming back to life?"

"Yes. It's an interesting phenomenon. The buying trends seem to be guided by the attitude of all the customers taken together. They dictate sales volume. It seems to have little to do with need. Many women have thirty-five outfits they can cobble together. Times get tough and these women switch the clothes around or wear the same ones more frequently."

"Just so," Meg said. "They know they can get by for a while. Many of them have loaded up their credit cards and when losing their job becomes a possibility, they pay off their balances and use cash and the occasional check. Just ask me."

"More attitude," Scott remarked. "I have no idea how much it has to do with what's going on in the economy."

When they were in Alexis' office, Scott took Meg's hand and said, "I hope you come back to us." When he had left the room, Meg turned to Alexis and asked to use the telephone. "I need to find out if I can have my old apartment back. If it's vacant it's a matter of bringing the stuff up from the basement."

After her short train trip from the city, Meg walked out of the station to the spot where she knew Rob would be waiting for her. He saw her coming and leaned over to open the door. After they had kissed, she said, "Rob, darling, I'm going back."

"In a way, I'm pleased for you, if not for me."

"I'll say it again, that you can return to the city with me and share the apartment you already know."

"I've had only a day to think about it, but in that time I've concluded that you belong back in your career. Let me guess that the time out here has been good for you. Your body's harder. You have new skills that you may never need again, but nonetheless new skills. And a man who is very appreciative of the few years we've been together."

"And how do you see the future for yourself, Rob?"

"I'm much better grounded than when you found me. I can make a new female contact, if I want. I can take Rose's offer seriously. I guess our children would like to see us together again, although they haven't been too vocal on the matter."

"Give me a few days to pull my possessions together and say goodbye to the neighbors and to the friends I've made at church."

"Take your time. Will you have the former apartment to move back to?"

"Yes. It's still vacant. I asked them to move my things back upstairs from the basement."

"I'll drive you into town. We should be able to fit your belongings into the back of the car."

In the evenings remaining they became eager lovers. Rob told Meg that it reminded him of the first week they lived together.

"That was discovery, finding one another. This may be farewell, using the occasion to make the best gift one can to the other," Meg said.

"I'm letting you go because birds in cages really would prefer to live in nature. It wouldn't do to keep you here when you want to be elsewhere."

The day came for Meg's departure. She took her few clothes and put them across the back seat of the car. He insisted she take the quilt she had worked on at the church and finished at home.

They were quiet on the drive into the city. He put his hand on the seat between them. She reached out and held it. "This is easy come, hard go," Meg said. "Tonight I'll be in my old bed with the quilt over me. I'll be sleeping alone instead of up against you. It will be a while before I regain my equilibrium."

"You can throw yourself into your work and in a month a new man might move into your life and solve those problems."

"Or create new ones," Meg said.

The farewell was brief. Rob inspected the apartment with its furniture in place. "Like you, it's warm and comfortable," he said.

He was back in his car and on the road before the evening traffic picked up. When he drove off the expressway, he pulled over and sensed that he was about to cry. He carried a box of tissues on the floor of the passenger side. He took out three tissues and allowed the tears to flow. He thought about what a wonderful woman she was and how much she had added to his life for the better part of four years. After some minutes the tears let up and he drove home. The aspects of life waiting for him were an unopened newspaper, the radio, a meal he would cook and a full bottle of red wine. He knew he would have to dig himself out of this hole, and he knew he had done the correct thing by encouraging Meg to resume her former life.

On her first day at work, Meg decided to wear the outfit that had served her well in the country: the white blouse and a colorful scarf. She went first to Alexis' office and told her that this was as well as she could manage on the first day and would be digging into her former wardrobe after work. Alexis told her that Scott had enjoyed their lunch together, that she had given Scott Meg's home telephone number, and that he would wait a month before asking her out.

"Did he want my telephone number, or did you force it on him?" Meg asked.

"He asked for it. He said you were a lovely person." Alexis paused, and then added, "He might be easy to hook."

"I've been able to hook them," Meg answered. "This time I want to hook the right one for keeps."

WAVES IN OUR LIVES
PART 13

Rob looked back on the first week without Meg and calculated that it was the worst week in his life except for those he had spent in Vietnam, about thirty weeks in combat out of the total of fifty-two weeks in the country. This feeling was different. There was no element of danger; it was a matter of looking forward to an empty life. Meg had provided all the warmth and comfort that a woman in love with him could. She was amusing and cheerful. She made no demands on him. He was surprised at the end that she had been contemplating a change for the last year of their life together.

He could scout women, he knew, and might find someone with whom he could be compatible, but it would not be a relationship as rewarding as his with Meg. He could not decide the part of her that was the most pleasing. It might be her conversation, or the ease with which she went about routine matters, or it could have been the delicious woman she was in bed.

The chance of finding a woman with Meg's appeal seemed remote, though miracles did happen, he knew. Rob reviewed the available women in his locale, all from church, and thought that two of them could open up to him and become satisfactory mates, but there were no guarantees. Meg had shown up one afternoon. There was no effort on the part of either one to create a working relationship. It was there from that first afternoon.

Then there was Rose. Her offer stood. She could buy a house, as she had indicated, and they could resume their life together. Rob thought it a bit cold blooded on her part to be living with Vince and at the same time making offers to him. Going back to Rose would solve two problems. First, she was a thoroughly acceptable partner. They had smoothed out the rough spots between them over the years. Second, she represented re-entry into city life. Perhaps he was tiring of life in the country, the sameness year to year, and the lack of excitement. His life without Meg would consist of familiar routines, each of which he knew by heart. Might there be advantages to returning to his former life? Back then his life was filled with people and events that injected newness and occasional excitement into his day-to-day affairs.

He would have to get beyond Rose and Vince and their love affair. On the other hand, Meg and he had had and enjoyed a substantial adventure. There was no difference except that he had left Rose for the countryside and precipitated all the events that came after. He accepted responsibility for those developments.

Meg had recounted to him what Scott had told her about the departure and eventual return to the department store of Philadelphia women, mostly from the Main Line. They had made their quiet exits during bad times only to resurface once the worst of the recession was over. He added those events to his evidence that important financial ups and downs do have an effect on the psychology of great masses of people. The downdraft may have started with weakness in the housing market, but the forces at work were amplified by the actions of millions of people curtailing their purchasing of all manner of objects not related to houses. Rob didn't know how he would fit this into his general theory of business cycles, but certainly it was a piece.

A third advantage of life in Philadelphia, lacking in his life in the country, was that he would have access to colleagues, some retired, others still active. One or more of these could introduce a point or a nuance that he had overlooked. For certain, many of them had contemplated the business cycle and drawn their own conclusions.

Rob knew that age was catching up with him and that sexual activity would provide less pleasure as his ability to perform decreased. He didn't know whether women were so afflicted. He had never discussed the matter with either Rose or Meg. When his prowess started to fail him he knew he ought to be established securely with a woman his age. It wouldn't do to be in the first stage of impotence as he was starting a relationship with a woman still in the grips of a strong appetite. Another reason to return to Rose, he thought.

The only person losing in these exchanges would be Vince, Rob knew. Meg had what she wanted, if it was only going back to work. She had mentioned a certain Scott who had taken her to lunch where he conducted his interview. Rob wondered where that relationship might lead, and whether this Scott interviewed male candidates in the same fashion.

Rob tried to look at matters in a new way. It was Rose who was giving up Vince. Little doubt that Vince had been getting his fill of her. It had been obvious to Rob that Vince cared deeply for Rose, even when Vince's wife was alive. Vince had had Rose all the time he, Rob, lived in the country. Perhaps that was Vince's quota and the time had come for him to start again in a new direction.

Rob waited two weeks to feel certain about what he was doing. Life alone, or life without Meg, made no sense. It became more obvious each day that he should explore Rose's offer. It was almost three weeks since he had driven Meg into the city with her few possessions, including her quilt. He thought that whenever he telephoned Rose it would be fifty-fifty whether he reached Rose or Vince. He placed the call mid-afternoon. Vince answered.

"Hello, Vince. It's Rob."

"I half expected that it would be you. Do you want to speak to Rose?"

"Yes, please, Vince." Rob had almost asked Vince what he meant by 'half-expected' and was glad he hadn't.

Rose came on the line promptly. She was sitting in the solarium. "I'm easy to find, Robby."

"Yes, you are. How are you?"

"Moderately well, thank you."

"I wanted to discuss the offer you made about cohabitation."

"Has Meg left you?"

"Yes, a little while ago. She was summoned back to work. She invited me to come along and rebuild my life in the city with her."

"Why did you turn her down?" Rose asked.

"Fifth wheel syndrome. I can't rebuild a life with her when you and I had an acceptable life in the city. Made no sense even though I hold her in the highest regard."

Rose said nothing so Rob continued. "You had said you might buy a house for us to live in."

"I am buying a house. I had to be honest and upfront with Vince. I told him that I had suggested that you and I pick up where we left off."

"And his response?"

"He was understanding and a bit distressed. I'm sleeping in the guest bedroom. No double bed is wide enough."

"And you said you were buying a house."

"Yes, working with a realtor. When I decide on an acceptable house, do you want to add your approval?"

"No. Your taste trumps mine. If your offer stands, I'll move in with you when you close on the house. When could that be?"

"One week or two or thereabouts."

"I'll have to pack two hundred days of canned fruits and vegetables. They are in one-quart glass containers at the moment."

"I'm sure we'll go through all of it. By the way, we have no furniture. Harriet took our house completely furnished."

"What did she do with her stuff?"

"Sold it, I guess. We'll have to start from scratch."

"New furniture would be good but I'm afraid we're destined for the used market," Rob said.

Rose bought furniture for the master bedroom and the kitchen. Her inheritance had been gone through in buying the house. Rob arrived on the same day Rose did and they were not surprised that they experienced a series of awkward moments. Emptying Rob's car of glass jars and moving them to the basement gave them something to do. Rose had ample dresses and suits to fill the closets and there were piles of her clothes on the floor that would go into a couple of dressers.

When they realized that the kitchen had no cooking utensils, they went to a used furniture and clothes store and bought the necessities. Following that they went to a supermarket, Rose making a list on the way. They stood in the empty living room, each holding a glass of wine. Finally they kissed.

"Quite some adventures we've had," Rose said.

They were both able to laugh at that moment. "I can't explain it," Rob said, "but I feel stronger for the experience. We both managed it."

WAVES IN OUR LIVES
PART 14

They thought after supper that it would be appropriate to telephone one of the children. If a visit was forthcoming, they would wait for the event to pass before telephoning the other, knowing that their children would discuss the news with one another.

Harriet, her husband and their child lived closer than their son, Stanton, who went by Stan. Rose and Rob had discussed their children in detail over the years, deciding that both were destined to be accomplished people. All the results were not in yet, the parents agreed.

The older child, Harriet, was approaching forty. She was a medical doctor, had elected to have one child, who turned out a boy and who was nearing his tenth birthday. This boy was named Robinson for his grandfather but in the family he was called Crusoe. The boy liked the name. He had an illustrated version of the text and would leaf through it with his grandfather as they discussed events. Rob never interrupted the boy to tell him that he was familiar with the story.

Rose and Rob were keen on the boy. He seemed to have the wit and warmth missing in his mother; the good qualities might have come in part from his father. Harriet had always wanted to be a medical doctor. She elected to be a surgeon and ended up specializing in fixing people's hearts. "There will not be many after me," she would say. Her belief was that the bleeding of patients, a procedure popular two centuries previously, showed how backward her profession was. "In a century, the idea of cutting into people with sharp objects will seem as barbaric as bleeding patients seems to us now." She was very successful, although young, and as far as Rose and Rob were concerned, cold as ice.

Harriet's husband, Stephen, started as a technical writer and was now the editor of the scientific journal where he had always worked. He pronounced his first name Steven but left the spelling as it was given to him.

Harriet's profession made her keep erratic hours, with the result that Stephen did most of the rearing of their son. Stephen would take Crusoe to the park, or to the zoo, or to have a picnic, while Harriet might be called away to the hospital on an emergency.

Rob telephoned Harriet and Stephen before calling their son Stan. Stephen came on the line. "Hello Rob. We got a call from Rose a couple of days ago telling us you were coming back. Welcome home."

"Thank you Stephen. Any chance of seeing you soon?"

"Tomorrow night, if that's not too soon. I'm cooking as I usually do. Harriet could be here or get here at any time, you can't tell."

"That's kind of you, Stephen. How's Crusoe?"

"He's doing well. Starting lacrosse this fall, which has him excited."

"Well, it will be good to see the three of you. Rose sends her best."

Rose and Rob arrived at six o'clock for dinner. They were greeted by Stephen and Crusoe. Harriet was in the operating room at her hospital. There were embraces all around, followed by drinks for the adults. "How was it out there?" Stephen asked. "A thing of beauty to live in the country and become absorbed in the elementary aspects of life," Rob answered.

Stephen was interested in Rob's routine and out of politeness to Rose refrained from any mention of Meg. He got around to asking about intellectual activities. "Did you carry on with Kondratiev?" he asked.

"He's never far away from me but I became preoccupied with everyday matters. Let me say that when someone provided fresh material I filed it away immediately."

"Do you think you'll get back to that topic?" Stephen asked.

"No question. I've considered contacting the University for a bit of space, an abandoned office perhaps. The intellectual climate could spur me on."

Harriet appeared half-way through dinner. "Another life saved," she announced. She took her place at the table and Stephen went to the kitchen to fetch a plate with warm food. In no time, Harriet said, "Well, you two have had your mid-life crises!"

"Harriet, we're too old for mid-life anything," Rose said.

"How about late-in-life flings?" Harriet asked.

"I think that more nearly describes events," Rose answered. She went on. "You two could keep the experience in mind. I think it's fair to say that it cleared the air for us."

Rob thought for a moment before adding, "People who experience one flavor all their lives may never know if it suits them."

Rose said right away, "Robby, I'm at least three flavors and you like them individually and you like them mixed together."

Rob had a vague notion of what his wife meant and let the matter rest.

Stephen introduced a new topic. "On the matter of the house, we couldn't have afforded anything beyond rent until Harriet became a full-fledged, highly paid surgeon. We were prepared to relinquish this place back to you on a moment's notice but you, Rose, announced that you would be buying a house before we could make any move. Now you've done it, thanks to your aunt's generosity, and I suppose that means we can stay. By the way, do you want the furniture back?"

"No. Rob and I are headed for the used furniture shops and the estate sales. Gives us something to do. We'll redo our wills and let you two have this place and Stan gets the house we just bought."

"That's thoughtful and generous. By my calculations Harriet and I have twenty-five years of living together and making mistakes before embarking on our late-in-life flings."

"I hope you do as well as we did," Rob said.

Rose and Rob were surprised at how easily they had reunited. There had been none of the rancor that can be caused by divorce. The property settlement to date had favored the daughter who had produced a grandson while the second house would go later on to the son and daughter-in-law who had not had children. Whether they wanted children was another matter. Stan and his wife Claudia were mum on the matter with the result that Rose and Rob had stopped speculating.

The evening went on, taking its normal course. Crusoe said a few words about lacrosse and how much he looked forward to starting the game. Stephen talked about the travel required of him in order to be the responsible editor of his technical journal. Harriet went to her favorite topic: the advances being made in the treatment of heart diseases. The emergency operation late that afternoon called on her to replace a valve in an otherwise healthy heart, the property of a well-know athlete now in his sixty-second year.

Crusoe had gone to bed. The two wine bottles were empty. Rob looked at Rose and nodded. Words were not required. The four of them stood and bade one another goodnight.

It was a short drive home. Rose volunteered that she had enjoyed herself and that Harriet had been more forthcoming than usual, even though she needed to make progress in the field of human relations.

"Remember, we are a dysfunctional family," Rob said.

"All families are dysfunctional," Rose answered.

WAVES IN OUR LIVES
PART 15

R ob telephoned his son Stan on the day following. Rose had talked to him previously to discuss the reconciliation. "Should we be glad for both of you?" Stan asked. "You may as well," his mother answered. "We're too old to separate again."

"Were there any good aspects to the experience?" Stan persisted. "Better to live with Vince than live alone those three plus years," she had answered.

On this telephone call, Stan was direct with his father, as he was with most everyone. "Yes, we want to see you soon. How about dinner here on Saturday?" Stan suggested.

Rob had reflected often during his time spent in the countryside how little he had seen of his children. The distance, as short as it was, could not have been an issue. The completely different life could be one reason, and after Meg arrived on the scene, his children might have found it difficult to replace their mother with this younger woman.

Rob felt that when he was with Rose, Harriet, Stephen, and Crusoe, social intercourse was simpler than when he and Rose were with Stan and Claudia. The existence of the fifth person made it possible to loosen conversation, to turn to the reactions of a child, and to expect humorous answers. When Rob and Rose were together with Stan and Claudia, there was but one mood, seriousness. Rob and Rose had expected a child or two to come along from this marriage, but that was not to be the case.

Stan, named for Stanton, Virginia, where a female forbearer stemmed from, had followed his father at the University and majored in his father's field of study. They differed in that Stan wanted to work on the financial pages of a newspaper. He found such a job and remained on the staff of the newspaper until his layoff, caught as he was in the downdraft of the print medium. Stan had despaired of finding work, the supply of major dailies being limited, but he continued writing in his field, selling an occasional piece, a few to his newspaper.

Stan was well aware of the great number of books on personal finance that the publishing houses had brought forth. He had made several outlines of ten-chapter books that he could write but had not been able to interest either a publisher or an agent. The publisher of his father's multiple-edition best seller told Stan that the firm handled only textbooks and had no interest in the popular market.

Over the years, Stan and his father had held several conversations concerning the advantages of graduate school. Stan could not deny his father's accomplishments but he maintained that he cared more for newspaper work than he did for teaching and research.

Until his layoff, Stan had no reason to question his choice of career, but after a couple of years of unemployment, he caved in. "I may be applying to graduate schools, Dad," he said when the four of them were sitting around the cocktail table before dinner. Perhaps Stan's vision of himself as a newspaperman held that he should drink the hard stuff, which he was drinking at that moment, and peck away at a portable typewriter when at work.

"You did well in your undergraduate years. I take it you are applying at our University," Rob said.

"Yes, I am, Dad."

"Well, if you're not accepted right away let me know and I'll go by Admissions. They're all so young over there; they could invite me to get lost."

"Thanks anyway, Dad. I hope that with a course or two behind me I could become an assistant, grade papers, teach a section, that sort of thing."

"I'm sure you could. Look into the journalism department as well. They might eat you up over there."

Rob turned to face Claudia. "What's new with you, dear one?" Claudia was not accustomed to answering direct questions and paused. Rose interceded and said, "I don't think Rob is after your dark secrets. Are you still working?"

"Yes. The high school needs to teach its kids the elements of computing so I continue to do that. Let me see how dinner is doing." With that Claudia escaped to the kitchen. Rose followed her, offering help.

Claudia and Stan had met at a community college. She was teaching the class and he was one of about twenty-five students learning the simple and complex functions of the two programs that he was using in his newspaper work. Stan had waited until the last four sessions when he started asking her out. She put him off until the end and she let him take her for a brief meal before driving her back to her car so that she could continue home.

Claudia was a beautiful woman of a few words. Stan did not speak a great deal himself. Rose and Rob wondered how they spent time together. They imagined that there were long stretches of silence interrupted by an occasional observation or question.

On their past drives to Stan and Claudia's place, Rose and Rob would hold the usual exchange to the effect that if they did most of the talking they would tend to reinforce Stan and Claudia's behavior. "Maybe 'Don't speak until spoken to' is not the correct thing to teach children," Rose had observed once. As a person who avoided repeating herself, she never said those words to Rob again.

It remained a mystery to Rob and Rose why Stan and Claudia attended the games of the professional teams in Philadelphia. When Stan lost his job there was less of it. The parents thought that Stan and Claudia had found an activity that they could share and be brought together by it.

At this dinner, Rob and Rose described the rewriting of their wills and the eventual disposition of the house they had just moved into. The introduction of financial matters brought Stan around to questioning his father on Kondratiev.

"Well, I keep at it. If you bring up business cycles to anyone you get a response. Everyone has an opinion."

"Will you be writing something soon, Dad?"

"Yes. I have a few people on my back on the subject, including your mother. I thought I could start by asking the head of my department for a little space. To be at the University would get me in the right mood."

"Do you sense your article will be earth-shaking?" Stan asked.

"No. It's a simple concept. I wouldn't get it published except that I have a publisher and a slightly recognized name. Of course the business cycle is big news now and that might help."

"How long will the article be?" Stan asked.

"I feel that I can say it all in a few thousand words." Then Rob added, "Get your job as a teaching assistant and we'll co-author the paper. I don't need the publication, obviously, but it might give you a lift."

"Are you putting me in charge of punctuation?" Stan asked.

"No. And no wise remarks. Let's see if you can organize material and prevent yourself from writing as a newspaperman would. We'll just be presenting simple concepts, no new research needed."

"We can block out the paper whenever you wish. Your place or mine? as they say," Stan asked.

On the way home, Rose commented that she had been on the receiving end of a few paragraphs from Claudia while they were in the kitchen. "She asked me what it was like to sleep with a different man after forty years."

"And how did you handle that?" Rob asked.

"I said that if you like the man, it is the right thing to do to satisfy a need. Then I asked her if Stan and she were happy in bed and happy in general together. She changed the subject."

"Maybe we should not expect confessions from those two," Rob said.

"They've been married quite a while and I would guess that they have been each other's only partner," Rose concluded.

WAVES IN OUR LIVES
PART 16

On the drive home, Rose asked Rob if he was serious about getting around to writing on Kondratiev.

"My only concern," he answered, "is that when you've finished your work on earth you curl up and die."

"People die from cancer and heart failure, Robby. They don't die from the lack of a life goal."

"Well, I've heard that the lack of just such a life goal causes a relaxation in the immune system and one of those dreadful diseases overwhelms your defenses, then it's just *kaput*."

"I've heard that too. Millions of women are not driven by life goals and outlive their men. Put that in your pipe and smoke it."

"Let's examine you. What have been your life goals, Rose?"

"Very simple, I'd say. I wanted to marry and have a couple of kids. Presently my mission is to be good to you, stay alive on this planet and keep circling the sun. We're both approaching seventy revolutions."

"If I finish on Kondratiev, Rose, I'll need some lesser goals. I have to do something to keep going," Rob said.

"I enjoy cooking, and gardening, and reading, and all the cultural activities we've been involved with over the decades. Any ideas there?" Rose asked.

"You didn't mention travel. Do you enjoy travel?"

"Yes, I do, but notice how pleasant it is to come home."

"Of course you couldn't experience that sensation without leaving home in the first place," Rob said.

"How true." They were quiet for a moment then Rose said, "I thought it was generous of you to invite Stan to co-author the paper. I think he would like to see his name in a professional journal next to his father's. It would be a bonding experience, I think."

"We may as well start; that way we can discover the repercussions of losing one's life goals. I'll telephone the University tomorrow."

"Robby, when you've written about the reasons for the business cycle, the psychological stuff as you call it, then you can go to work on whether people who finish their life's work die sooner than those who stretch it out. That would make a great life goal. You could make yourself last a long time."

"Are you telling me, Rose, that I can live until I'm one hundred and twenty?"

"No, silly. You've made this assertion and I think you need data to back it up. In any event, you should be able to live just as long as I will."

"That's fair," Rob said. "Stan and I will write about the business cycle, and then I'll research life cycles. If it lets me live as long as you do, so much the better."

That was part of their conversation on Saturday evening. On Sunday afternoon they gardened and as they were kneeling and weeding, Rob turned to Rose and said, "You know as well as I do that I'm in decline and that in five years or so I might not be able to satisfy you."

"Yes, Robby, I know about that phenomenon and I guess that the existence of pills to fight off erectile dysfunction says it all."

"Don't you love the term, erectile dysfunction? We used to say that you couldn't get it up any longer."

"That being the case, let's not waste too many evening," Rose said.

"Which brings up another topic," Rob said. "Do women have the equivalent of erectile dysfunction? That is, after a while are they incapable of having an orgasm?"

"I don't know the answer to the question. Women seem not to confide in one another on the subject. I can tell you speaking for myself that there is a gentle decline after menopause."

"The pharmaceutical companies had better invent pills for women. We'll call them pleasure pills," Rob said.

"So, Robby, there's another topic to examine, but I won't let you go door to door for your data. The women might invite you in. I'd think that after you've finished with the business cycle and the life cycle you can start on the pleasure cycle, but do it from home."

"Rose, you're pulling my leg but it sounds like an interesting investigation. I could start with you."

"That's a very useful idea, darling." It was the first time she had used that particular term of endearment since he had returned.

The day following, Monday, Rob telephoned the head of his former department for an appointment. Rob had held that post for five years during his fifties. The new head of the department would see him that afternoon, if that was convenient.

Free office space was not available but a small, vacant office could be given to him if he would act in an official capacity. One task was to be the thesis advisor to several students working on their doctorates. The second was to conduct seminars on topics in his field. Well-known professors and individuals who practiced economics in the business world would conduct two-hour discussions on their subject. Rob accepted both positions as he had nothing much to do now that he was no longer farming. A small stipend went along with the positions. He telephoned his son and they set a time for their first meeting.

In this meeting, held at the student union over coffee, father and son outlined their paper. They established the stages of the business cycle as follows: 1. Steady State; 2. Enthusiasm; 3. Euphoria; 4. Burst Bubble; 5. Decline; and 6. Recovery. These six stages of the business cycle would be shown to result from shifts in the outlooks of masses of citizens, slowly altering their behavior. They thought they might not be able to demonstrate cause and effect without any doubts remaining, but at least they would show associations.

Rob asked his son whether he felt knowledgeable in the field of psychology and when Stan said that he was familiar with the terms used in the popular press, they decided that they could look for definitions when the appropriate time had come as they wrote about each of the six segments.

They elected to start right then and there, both being equipped with paper and pen. Rob noticed that Stan was warming to the task.

They started with the Steady State. These would be the years when serious, commonsensical persons would be at the helm of business and governmental matters. Over-expansion of either would be held in check by the sober behavior of those in charge. The movers and shakers, always present, would be stymied, and checkmated, as they were shown to be a dangerous element in the conduct of an economy. The graphs generated by Kondratiev did not have plateaus or flat areas that Rob could point to and say, "Aha, Steady State," but there were flat areas between the peaks and valleys. They would do.

Stan suggested they examine the charts constructed by Kondratiev, and pick out by decades the Steady State portions of the charts from the earliest ones in the time of Napoleon. "We ought to assure investors that the Steady State exists. Should we tell them why each period terminates?"

"Good thinking, Stan," Rob said. "The answer to your question goes to the meat of the article, how the changes in the national mood drive the Kondratiev curves up and down."

Rob said that he would get out his collection of Kondratiev graphs and determine the dates of the Steady State portions as best he could. Stan volunteered that he would go to the library and take out one or more texts on psychology in search of appropriate terms.

Their next meeting was held in Rob's new office. It was large enough to hold a desk, two chairs, a file cabinet, and a book case. They went over the material gathered to date and started work on the next section, titled tentatively, Enthusiasm.

When they were fifteen minutes into the topic, Stan said to his father, "We settled on six periods in our business cycle. I'm voting that we review Euphoria and make certain that Peak is part of it. Peak is just a moment, say a day or a week in the midst of Euphoria, but readers will be looking for it."

Rob thought about it for a moment and said, "I need sustenance. Off it is to the student union for lunch, coffee and a refill." Over their sandwiches they added Peak to Euphoria, agreeing that readers would be looking for that all-important moment.

When they had finished lunch, Stan turned to his father and asked him a question that had been on his mind. "Do you think that it was inevitable, this enormous downdraft we've suffered through?"

"Frankly, I do, Stan," his father answered "The difference between me and many others is that I believe in Kondratiev while the others have only heard of his theory. Belief is strong. When you believe in something you act on it. I believe in Kondratiev and the belief made me move into the country and learn to grow food. The situation did not become so dire that segments of society collapsed, but I thought it would come to that."

"They're saying now that we can assign much of the blame to the subprime mortgage mess. Does that take the edge off Kondratiev?" Stan asked.

"No. We believers say that every fifty or sixty years disaster strikes and you must start over. If it hadn't been subprime mortgages it would have been something else. Folly was in the air."

"The other day," Stan said, "you proclaimed the years 2007 and 2008 as the years we reached bottom. Shall we add fifty to sixty years and keep on the lookout for 2058 to 2059?"

"You and I will not be present but I should write a letter to Crusoe, a time capsule of sorts. He will be entering his late middle age and would appreciate advice from his grandfather. You may as well sign the letter with me."

"They will be analyzing these events for years to come," Stan said.

"Yes, that's true. Plenty to mull over," his father answered. "Did you by any chance get to read *Fool's Gold*?"

"Yes, I did. I was still employed at the time, 2009, I recall, and the newspaper would receive these publications on the gamble that we would write a review of them. I may very well have written the review of *Fool's Gold*. I enjoyed the book. Written by Gillian Tett, a British newspaper woman. It presented a history of the development of the new banking culture. I liked the glossary in the back of the book. You could always turn to it and understand what you were reading."

"Had I written the book," Rob observed, "the closing chapter would have been on the Kondratiev Waves. I'll bet my ten acres that we were due for a collapse, mortgages or no mortgages."

WAVES IN OUR LIVES
PART 17

After they had finished their sandwiches and were on a second cup of coffee, Rob asked Stan, "When you write an article, how do you start out?"

"If you recall a few articles of mine, you see that I choose a short sentence covering a thought familiar to the reader. In our case I'd say that each phase of the business cycle is driven by activities that have taken place in the previous phase. That shouldn't scare off a reader."

"Not in the least. Seems obvious, in fact," Rob said.

"That's the idea. Write something obvious that the reader agrees with. In our case, Recovery comes just before Steady State so I'd write that during Recovery the government tightened regulations, slowed the expansion of credit, cleaned up the balance sheets of banks, and conducted a purge of bad debt hiding here and there."

"That's a very good start, Stan. Where do you go from there?"

"Because we want to introduce the psychological factors, I would go to the mood swings in the country. That would be my next paragraph, how the national mood changed because of the actions of the government to find the problems and fix them."

"That's perfect, Stan. We have to do that for each of the six segments. Remember we tossed out Peak when we decided Peak was simply a week or so inside of Euphoria."

"That's right, Dad. Along the same line, how would you handle the phase, Enthusiasm?"

"When a large segment of the population becomes bored with Steady State, the bored ones advocate more risk-taking, more action, more and better schemes to make money, the time when many people expect wealth to be created in a hurry. Yes, more credit cards, more car sales, more real estate activity, more initial public offerings, and all the markets rise except for the price of oil."

"And it happened the way you describe it, Dad. Many people in the population were making money during Enthusiasm."

"I didn't think it was sustainable," Rob said. "Systems are not meant to expand at a great rate. You're held in check by increases in the population and the increased productivity of the average worker. If you try to expand beyond those limiting factors, something has to give," Rob said.

"You're conservative at heart," Stan told his father.

"That's true. They say that old people become conservative. What they leave out is that old people have lived through the business cycle and it's hard to fool them."

"Enough philosophy," Stan said. "Let's move on to Euphoria. Maybe I'll lead off on this one. I'm young and have sinned against the system."

"You don't have an expensive mortgage, that's a plus," Rob said.

"Yes, but Claudia and I got in over our heads with credit cards. We've learned our lesson and cut back to one each, which we pay off each month."

"All good news," Rob said.

"Anyway, Euphoria is characterized by large blocks of the population believing that the good times will roll on forever. Most everybody is in denial. No need to save—I'll win the lottery. I want it all now because I deserve it. You know all the folly, Dad."

"Yes, I know it. How can you help not knowing it? That's why I moved out to the country and learned to grow vegetables. Turned out I overdid it, but I'm cautious by nature. Until Meg showed up your mother was always welcome to join me. I expected society to unravel, but of course that wasn't the case. I overdid it."

"Well, it's your turn on Euphoria, Dad. Do you want to add to what I've said?"

"Sure. The final stage. Almost the entire society has gone nuts. The undergirding psychological factor is that ninety percent of the country thinks that everything is going up forever: the value of their house, their income, the value of their investments, the stock market, their disposable income, and so on. Of course it's not true. Nothing lasts forever. A hyperactive system, as ours got to be, doesn't need much to derail it. They say now that it was an over-expanded credit market, adjustable rate mortgages, over-loaded credit cards, insufficient government regulations, you name it. Of course they were right. The fact that these dangerous situations existed all at once meant that if one or more was attacked, the entire system could grind to a halt. And that's what happened."

"How long would you say that Euphoria lasted, Dad?"

"Hard to say, exactly. But as I've mentioned, the bulk of Euphoria took place in two years, 2007 and 2008. That should cover it."

"And how about the Burst Bubble, what's your take on that," Stan asked.

"Well, a few people saw a dark cloud on the horizon. They sold their holdings in the stock market. A few more people who were selling their homes had to cut the asking price. Suddenly there's an increase in the number of personal bankruptcies, followed by a mad rush for the exits and people, great masses of people, get religion and promise that never again will they do risky things. Mattresses are stuffed with legal tender. Economic activity slows on all levels, that's a Burst Bubble."

"And this newspaperman lost his job," Stan reflected. Then he added, "I would want to say through no fault of my own, but let's face it, Claudia and I were wallowing in debt along with the rest of them."

They sat silently, each occupied with his thoughts. Then Stan asked his father, "What about the period of Decline?"

"Retrenchment at various speeds. Terribly difficult period," Rob answered. "It's as though an airplane flew over and pink slips floated down like confetti. Lasts quite a while. We have been through the worst of it. These are the months and years when the damage that was caused is repaired. Governments are busy. Companies are streamlining and individuals sliming down, finding out that it's possible to get through life with less. Quite an adjustment, but after all, the system needs this tightening of the belt."

"And as you say, Dad, each phase leads into the next one so when we are done with Decline, we step automatically into Recovery because the national mood is saying the system has corrected its faults during Decline and is now ready to advance to and through Recovery."

"That's right, Stan. That's the business cycle. I don't believe anyone will repeal it as long as there are humans who, by definition, know how to make a mess of everything and know how to clean up after themselves. By the way, Stan, I've written a new tax code. The tentative title is 'A Tax Code you Might Like.' If you want to we can co-author it. I haven't the vaguest idea who might publish it."

"One thing at a time, Dad. I'll read it, gladly, then we'll find a publisher, and by the way, what do you want to tell me about Meg?"

"Not much to say. This is strictly between you and me. Your mother would kill me if she got wind of any of this."

"That's the understanding, Dad."

"I left your mother for the countryside believing that life as we knew it would end and that food would be scarce. Your mother said that if I moved to the country our marriage would be over because she wasn't coming along. I didn't believe one word of it. She let a weekend pass without me and moved in with Vince who had been lusting over your mother for two decades."

"I knew that generally, Dad, but not in any detail."

"After nearly a year on my own, Meg came wandering down our road. She stopped first at the neighbors, the Gunthers, who sent her to me to get food. She had left Philadelphia after being let go and running out of money. What a free spirit! She came into my place and immediately I fed her, gave her the guest room, and let her have the first of innumerable hot showers. From those first moments it was a delightful escapade."

"Did she take you to bed, or did you have to mount a campaign?"

"Her exact words were, 'I'll leave my door ajar.' She was my lover for about three years. Or perhaps I was hers. You've heard of binge drinking? Well, this was the same thing, but in a different line of work. I know Vince well and I must tell you that between your mother and me, I had the better deal."

Rob wondered whether the time had come to ask Stan about his marriage. It just came out. "How well do you and Claudia get along, Stan?"

"From the outside you don't see it. You and Mom were and continue to be wonderful parents but you are limited by the material you have to work with. I was a lonely, quiet boy, perhaps introverted. With Claudia, I'm never alone. She understands. I'm never alone. She fills my life. What else can I say?"

"That tells me a lot," Rob said. "I guess you should be the one to polish the article. I have a bit more to do. As a matter of professional courtesy, I have to write a few paragraphs about another contributor to the subject of the business cycle. There's an important economist, Wesley Clair Mitchell, who earned his PhD at the University of Chicago in 1899 and gave the second half of his career to studying and writing on the business cycle. There's something to be said for obtaining your doctorate at the same university where you have your teaching career. You may have that experience. Other Chicago people were Arthur Burns, who became Fed Chairman, Milton Friedman, Thorstein Veblen, and so on. Some taught, others received their education there, some both.

Rob went on. "In 1925, Kondratiev and his wife came to the United States and met the economists who were studying and writing on the business cycle. I understand he was offered a teaching position here in the States."

"I wonder why he didn't accept the offer." Stan said.

"He had to leave at least a daughter in the Soviet Union. Stalin liked having the ransom right at hand," Rob answered.

"What about the inflation we're experiencing?" Stan asked.

"Unpredictable. We're at 80% total since 2009, when the big deficits kicked in," Rob answered.

"Do you think it will be Germany in 1925, wheelbarrows to cart your cash to buy groceries?"

"Hyperinflation. It wipes out everything. We may be heading that way. Notice I still hold on to my place in the country and go out there once a month with your mother to check on it. And of course, I've kept the wheelbarrow."

FICTIONAL KONDRATIEV CURVE

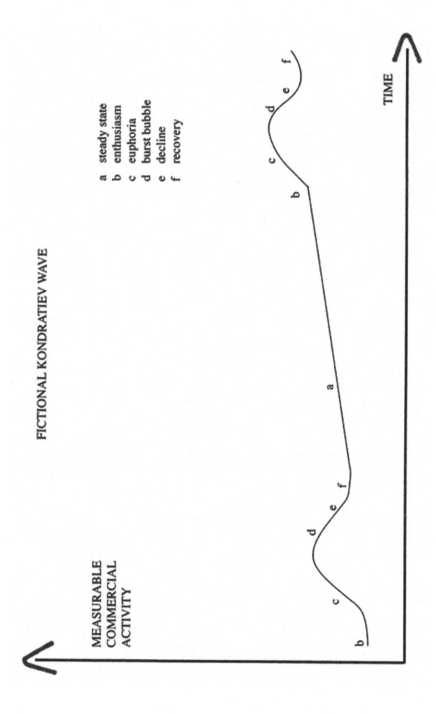

FICTIONAL KONDRATIEV WAVE

MEASURABLE COMMERCIAL ACTIVITY

TIME

a   steady state
b   enthusiasm
c   euphoria
d   burst bubble
e   decline
f   recovery

109

A TAX CODE
YOU MIGHT
LIKE

A Tax Code You Might Like
PART 1

"Dad, now that we have done with Kondratiev, I'm looking forward to jumping into your tax code. I have enjoyed what I've read. Where is it presently?"

"I think I've written a passable first draft, cleaned it up, and have passed it around to fellow professors. That would have been a little while ago," Rob said.

"What were their reactions; do you recall?" Stan asked.

"They admired the simplicity of the plan. I didn't do as well with the House of Representatives as I did with my colleagues."

"How so?"

"I know our member of the House. He would get in touch with me from time to time to sound me out on government spending. He had a seat on the House Ways and Means Committee, and I suppose he still does."

"What was his take on your ideas?" Stan asked.

"He said that they made sense but that they wouldn't fly, and his reason was simple enough. Once you have granted favors to sections of the public, it's difficult to take them away. He gave as an example the deduction we put on Schedule A for the interest we pay on our mortgage."

Stan added, "Perhaps another reason is that your new tax code forces many who do not pay taxes presently to start paying something. As you would create many, new taxpayers, your representative friend could see defeat at the next election. They may not pay taxes but they still vote," Stan said. He added, "Why don't we go over some of your main points, Dad?"

"The main point is to get rid of all the exceptions and thereby reduce the rates, keeping income to the Treasury the same," Rob said. He carried on. "What I've written sounds simple enough. Start at the top of the 1040 and you see right away that social engineering is important to people who write the tax code. Tax payers are divided into several categories, as though it were any one's business. We are made to declare whether we are filing our tax information as a married couple, or as a single person, or as head of household or a qualifying widow(er)." "Let me interrupt," Stan said. "What does 'head of household' mean?"

"Head of household consists of a single person with at least one dependent, a child as an example," Rob answered.

"That would include the young, divorced crowd. There are millions in that category," Stan said.

"Right away it's no longer an income tax," Rob continued. "The tax you pay depends in part on what you are doing in life. Married people join their incomes rather than paying taxes on their own earnings. In my plan, all who earn taxable income report it and pay their own taxes."

"How did Mom react to that?"

"She liked it. She said the present system must make some women, at least those that earn about what their husbands earn, feel like appendages. They are not sufficiently important to file a return of their own." Rob paused and then added, "Of course the two people that make up a married couple have the right to file as single individuals under the current version of the code but they end up paying more in taxes than they would filing as a married couple."

"I can imagine," Stan said, "that the so-called marriage penalty vanishes in your code when all individuals with income file their own returns."

"Exactly right. Goodbye marriage penalty. Let me continue. Currently we have personal exemptions and standard deductions. All they accomplish is to shield some of your taxable income with the result that the tax rates must go up. It does not take a gifted mathematician to grasp that shielding income from taxation forces the rates to go up in order to maintain the flow into the Treasury at a certain level."

"I haven't thought much about it," Stan said, "but whenever the administration, no matter which one it is, wishes to implement a new program they go right to the tax code, be it the IRA, or health savings accounts, or educational accounts. That must screw up the tax code."

"That's a nice, direct way to put it, Stan. I'm glad you have that reaction. It will make it easier working together."

"Dad, I'm aware of personal exemptions. Claudia is the wage earner in our small family now and when we do our taxes, we take two personal exemptions, one for each. Saves us plenty of money."

"Of course it does, but all taxpayers in your situation take the two personal exemptions as well, keeping the tax rates higher than they might be otherwise."

They fell silent, and then Rob introduced another aspect. "The couples with many children distort the system. Say there are six children, then there are eight personal exemptions, shielding a vast amount of money from taxation. The significance is that couples who chose not to have children, or cannot have children, or whose children are old enough to no longer be their dependants, must subsidize the parents with large number of children. It happens that the population of the United States has grown out of proportion to the ability of the land, air and water to support it. At least that's my opinion. The tax code, on the other hand, encourages creating more babies."

"Claudia and I have discussed that aspect of the code. It has always seemed unfair to us," Stan said.

Rob saw his chance. "In your case, was it that you couldn't have any?"

"I would say so," Stan answered. "We didn't seek medical advice, deciding that we would accept whatever came along. It turned out that one of us, we don't know which, was not able to reproduce and we accepted the verdict. We were philosophical about it, I would say."

"Your mother and I have always wondered," Rob said.

Perhaps to change the subject, Rob didn't know, Stan pointed at a folder that Rob had brought along that was on the desk. "Anything in that folder that has to do with the tax code?" Stan asked.

"Yes, the paper itself, along with notes," Rob answered. He opened the folder and turned over the title page and a table of contents, then picked up the first few sheets.

"What's your introduction?" Stan asked.

"I've always admired Andrew Mellon. He gave us the National Museum of Art on Constitution Avenue in the District of Columbia and he was Secretary of the Treasury under Harding,

Coolidge and Hoover. He wrote a slim volume on taxation and I start the article on the tax plan by quoting from that short treatise of his." Rob handed the sheets to Stan, who read what follows.

"The problem for government is to fix the rates which will bring a maximum amount of revenue to the Treasury and at the same time bear not too heavily on the taxpayers or on business enterprises. A sound tax policy must take into consideration three factors. It must produce sufficient revenue for the Government; it must lessen, so far as possible, the burden of taxation on those least able to bear it; and it must also remove those influences which might retard the continued steady development of business and industry on which, in the last analysis, so much of our prosperity depends. Furthermore, a permanent tax system should be designed not merely for one or two years nor for the effect it may have on any given class of taxpayers, but it should be worked out with regard to conditions over a long period and with a view to its ultimate effect on the prosperity of the country as a whole."

Rob and Stan continued discussing the present tax code and covered approximately these points.

Andrew W. Mellon, Secretary of the Treasury at the time, wrote the above as the opening paragraph of his book: *Taxation: The People's Business,* (The MacMillan Company, 1924). The purpose of the book was to persuade readers and particularly members of the Senate and the House of Representatives that the surtaxes (high taxes on personal income) put in place to finance the costs of World War I should be reduced. By 1924, half the debt incurred to cover wartime expenses had been paid off. Mr. Mellon made the arguments in his text that not only had the purpose of the high tax rates vanished, but also that the desired effect of the high rates had vanished as well. That is to say, individuals with high incomes had adjusted, in legal fashion, to the high rates and paid less and less year after year. Mr. Mellon asked that there be no rate higher than 25% on ordinary income.

Mr. Mellon got his tax cuts. Revenue to the Treasury went up. Similarly, President Kennedy reduced taxes during his tragically abbreviated term in office. Revenues went up. President Reagan reduced the tax rates when in office and revenues went up. The record shows that when surtaxes are eliminated and rates are taken down to a reasonable level, revenues to the Treasury increase. Professor Arthur Laffer dignified this body of evidence by plotting the data. We call this graph the Laffer Curve. The curve says that if the tax rate is zero, there will be no income to the Treasury, and if the tax rate is 100%, income to the Treasury will also be zero. The curve, which looks like a parabola, or the flight of a home run ball, tells us that there is a top tax rate that produces maximum income to the Treasury. Mr. Mellon thought that rate was 25%. Following this argument, President Clinton, in 1993, might have cut rates rather than increase them in order to bring more money into the Treasury.

Mr. Mellon's book is of the type one does not see these days. It is small. The type is large. There are but 229 pages. The pages measure five inches by seven-and-one-half inches. In hard cover, it weighs but twelve ounces. There is no jargon. It can be read easily in two sittings and understood completely by a person with no training in either economics or the theory of taxation. One regrets that it is out of print and must be borrowed from books in storage at a large library or from a special library.

Stan interrupted his father to ask him where he might find a copy of Andrew Mellon's book. Rob had answered, "There are several copies in the economics library. As a graduate student you can check one out." They continued their discussion of the tax code and a few historical matters. When the United States got underway in 1789, there were no taxes on the individual. Article 1, Section 9, of the Constitution prohibited such taxes. "No Capitation, or other direct, Tax shall be laid, unless in Proportion to the Census or Enumeration herein before directed to be taken." Because the government needed only $10,000,000 (ten million dollars) to operate year by year, the sum could be raised for the most part by customs duties. There were three million souls in America at the time, so the government operated on about three dollars per person per year. Two hundred twenty years later, the federal government requires $6,600 per person per year to operate. Divide the amount spent per year, two trillion dollars, by the number of inhabitants, three hundred million, to arrive at this figure. The government raises five-sixths of this $6,600 through taxation and borrows the remainder. To raise $6,600 per person per year, the government must tax incomes, capital gains, corporate profits, rents, dividends, interest, estates, gifts, alcohol, tobacco, gasoline, manufactured goods, and airline tickets (partial list). All the taxes listed above are allowed under the Constitution as adopted in 1787 with the exception of the income tax, which became legal in 1913 with adoption of the XVI Amendment. The right to tax estates is neither prohibited nor allowed in the Constitution. It is treated as an excise tax.

There have been three phases in the policy of taxation in the United States. In the first phase, from the founding to the start of the twentieth century, the individual was left alone, protected by the Constitution. There were no taxes on income, corporate profits, or estates. In the second phase, 1900 to 1920, taxes on income, corporate profits, and estates came into being and with them the concept of the ability to pay. The ability to pay became part of the tax code with the rates of taxation increasing as income went up. This is the progressive feature of taxation, which might vanish if a flat tax were in use. The ability to pay was not a new idea at the time. It appears as the first of Adam Smith's four guiding principles on taxation, which he enumerated in the *Wealth of Nations* (1776). "The subjects of every state ought to contribute towards the support of the government, as nearly as possible, in proportion to their respective abilities, that is, in proportion to the revenue which they respectively enjoy under the protection of the state."

The third phase, which is with us now in the first decades of the 21st century, originated during the New Deal. In this phase, the concept of the ability to pay is preserved and a new notion, the distribution of wealth, was added. The ability to pay is evidenced in graduated tax rates: the larger the income, the higher the tax rate. Distribution of wealth occurs when the taxes paid in by one individual are paid out to a second individual. Perhaps the earliest example of the distribution of wealth by the federal government appeared in the workings of the Social Security system. It started paying at the onset, in the late 1930s, a more substantial benefit to a low-income person who had paid in a small amount to the system, than to a high-income person who paid in a large amount to the system. Now, in 2012, the distribution of wealth by the federal government appears to be an unquestioned practice with near-unanimous following. All the social programs of the federal government enacted since the inauguration of Social Security in 1935 could not exist except for the taxing and spending policies incorporating the distribution of wealth.

If there is a single reason that permits the existence of a government that consumes at least 20% of Gross National Product, supports a massive federal debt, and creates budget deficits year after year, that reason is the belief held by a majority of elected officials that the distribution of wealth is acceptable and should be accomplished through taxation and additional spending by the federal government.

"That's a good start, Dad. Do you simply go through the 1040 and clean it up?"

"Yes, and I keep an eye on the business cycle. The tax code I've written would tend to flatten the Kondratiev curve we happen to be living through."

"How so, Dad?"

"Because vast numbers of new taxpayers would be created by the new code. They would keep their eyes on government spending and might curb that terrible urge on the part of elected people to spend, spend, spend,"

"Many of those new taxpayers could turn into angry voters if the out-of-control spending continued," Stan said.

A Tax Code You Might Like
PART 2

Rob and his son Stan were going over Rob's unpublished paper describing a tax code that Rob had drawn up.

"Yes, Stan, that's about it. I like your choice of verb, clean it up."

"You've knocked out marital status and the listing of dependents; what's next?" Stan asked.

"The W-2 needs revision. In a fantastic rip-off, the government takes 6.2% of your earned income, of your wages, up to some maximum amount, now over $100,000. That's your Social Security contribution. Then they take 1.45% of all your W-2 earnings. That's your Medicare contribution. What I dislike intensely about these deductions is that after taking them, you are required to pay ordinary income tax on these two deductions combined. I would think they would subtract these contributions from earned income before calculating the tax. Double dipping, I call it."

"Well, Dad, the elected officials are interested mainly in revenue. If the public doesn't scream about it, there will be no action taken."

"Right you are, Stan, but I have a trade to offer. As you know, the medical insurance your employer purchases for you comes to you tax free. It's not treated as income. I'm suggesting that the Social Security and Medicare contributions be subtracted from ordinary income and the cost of the medical insurance be substituted. In many cases the exchange would balance out, keeping revenue to the Treasury about the same."

"If revenue doesn't change, why bother?" Stan asked.

"Eliminate the rip-off of taxing your contributions to Social Security and Medicare, and then I'd like to force the employees to be aware of the cost of the medical insurance that the employer provides them. If the employees see how much tax must be paid on the insurance, then pressure might mount to lower the cost of the insurance funded by the employer."

"Dad, you live in a world of high hopes. Can you see elected officials making the cost of medical insurance taxable when they don't have to? After all, they have been taxing Social Security and Medicare contributions since the first day and no one has squawked."

"Perhaps, Stan, no one squawks because everyone uses a tax preparer and in the process taxpayers have become isolated from that reality. Perhaps I should have said inured to it."

"Inured is the correct word, Dad. Our system has become desensitized to the issue." They were silent for a moment, and then Rob continued.

"I have to believe that one person can make a difference, that a movement can be started with a well-written technical paper. If many of us did not believe that, change for the better would be difficult to come by."

"Well," Stan said, "you have my vote and Claudia's as well. She has a wonderfully clear mind, as you know."

Stan went off on a different tack. "I've read that there is a movement advocating the substitution of a national sales tax for the income tax, something similar to the Value Added Tax they use in Europe. What do you think of using a VAT?"

"It's a perfectly fine idea," Rob answered. "The difficulty would be to get the current income tax repealed while the VAT is being introduced. There's no doubt in my mind that urgent, compelling reasons would be found to keep both taxes in place, at least temporarily. And you know that a temporary tax would survive the life of our nation. Elected officials do not have the courage to repeal a tax completely."

"You mean that it would take the end of the United States to kill off one of the two taxes?" Stan asked.

"Yes, although in theory it's a fine idea. But I should make another point before we get back to the 1040, and that is to discuss the adjectives used by many writers and speakers when they describe a tax code. One is 'fair' and the other is 'practical.' Fairness means there is no tolerance for tax avoidance by the rich and it should mean the same for the poor and middle income citizens. Adam Smith was correct. Every citizen should contribute according to his or her ability. To foist off the entire responsibility of operating the government on a segment of the population, the rich, is unfair in the opposite direction. Do you agree to that, Stan?"

"Yes, easily. So does Claudia. We've talked about it."

"I don't mean to spend too much time on this, but I'm surprised that the Lefties, who pride themselves in being fair, would allow themselves to place such a high reliance on the rich and their checkbooks in order to finance governments. I am not aware of any definition of fairness that advocates forcing the top earners of a country to finance the operations of the government, without a strong assist from the balance of the population."

Stan was not certain his father had said all he had on his mind on the topic. He remained still. Rob did indeed have more to say. "Note that Andrew Mellon and Adam Smith suggest that citizens, to the extent possible, contribute to the operation of the government. And just one more idea. When the tax rates are too high, high earners make adjustments. A few of them leave the country. And note there is a migration within the fifty states by the rich from high-tax states to low-tax states. Tells you something, that people can and do make adjustments when circumstances turn against them. The elected people seem not to comprehend the phenomenon."

Stan waited a moment and said, "We got off track a bit, but what you just said had to be said. Fairness vanishes when a small percentage of the country does most of the heavy lifting and half the population pays nothing."

Rob waited and nodded in agreement. "I think we were talking about practicality as it applied to tax codes." And then he went to his main point, practicality. "You can't introduce the ability to pay at every time a tax is due. It's not practical. Your renewal at the DMV, bridge tolls, what you pay at the supermarket, or any store—there's no means test applied. And the most visible is the sales tax in those states that have one. That's a flat tax of 7%, let's say. Everyone is charged the same. All these are examples of practicality in taxation. In some instances, the practicality might be at the expense of fairness but you may not be able to have both simultaneously. There's a noun that I have left out and that's 'simplicity'. You reach simplicity in a tax code when the bulk of taxpayers can file their taxes without the help of a paid preparer. Let's say the new 1040 had no more than twenty lines. The last time I looked there were over seventy lines on the 1040, and plenty of forms to back up the calculations that go to each line."

"Give me an example of complexity, Dad."

"Well, here's an easy one. You contribute to your IRA. The amount of your contribution that you are allowed to deduct from taxable income decreases with rising income and very soon goes to zero. You can make the contribution, but you are not allowed to deduct it from taxable income. Here's another example. In my case as a retired person, I can receive social security payments but as my income goes up, the amount received that must be taxed as ordinary income keeps going up and peaks at 85% of the payments. And those are not scary complications. There are plenty worse," Rob added.

"Standardize the calculations; cut out the sliding scales; eliminate the exceptions. That's what I'm advocating," Rob said.

"The next section of the 1040 is income. What's your take on that, Dad?"

"The tax writers did well. They included all the forms of income so that one occupation is not favored over the other. As an example, if the receipt of rent were not taxed, everybody would want to own an apartment building. You get the picture."

"Makes sense, but I know you will have a comment because a refrain I've heard from you all my life is that there are always exceptions," Stan said.

"And that applied in this case. I have comments on the treatment of dividends and capital gains. Both should have their own treatment, as they have currently, and it should stay that way. The second Bush president made a change to the taxation of dividends. Dividends were always taxed twice; first, they were taxed as corporate income and then again as personal income on the part of the person to whom the dividend was paid. Dividends still are paid by a corporation after the corporation calculates its taxes on earnings. The dividend, if any, is distributed to shareholders and another tax is paid, admittedly smaller than before. Whether it was President Bush, or his advisors, or the tax writers in the Hill, I don't know, but the error was to require dividends to be paid after corporate taxes were paid. An incentive to pay out dividends was not created. So as it stands, the corporations do not benefit except to the extent that their shareholders admire their boards of directors. Admittedly the recipients of the dividends pay less income tax on the dividend received than they did previously."

"How would you have handled it, Dad?"

"I would have allowed the corporations to expense the dividend so that those corporations that do pay dividends have reduced earnings and they therefore pay less in corporate tax, and leave the rate of taxation as it always had been for the recipients of the dividends. Let dividends be an expense to the corporation. Let dividends be treated as ordinary income by the recipients, perhaps with its own tax rates. In other words, tax dividends just once. That way there exists an incentive for corporations to pay dividends. As it stands there is little if any incentive."

"I suppose where your argument falls down is that under your plan corporate tax payments are reduced for corporations that pay dividends, and the tax writers on the Hill are not disposed to let that happen," Stan said.

"I suppose you are right, but the best thing to happen to the United States would be to repeal taxes on corporations. What a boon that would be to the economy."

"Yes, but we have a ready chorus to tell us that it would be another giveaway to the fat cats. However, incomes would go up and unemployment would go down under your plan, and I might still have my job," Stan said.

"You have such clear thoughts for a young man, Stan. But getting back to where we were, I have comments on setting the tax rates on capital gains. The emphasis on the material you read is how much people should be allowed to keep on the sale of an asset. The social engineers are out there with their class warfare, spouting off about how the rich are getting richer and the poor are getting poorer, when all the time the discussion should be on how to make the pie larger. The social engineers want to take from the rich and give to the poor. The old, conservative Americans want to leave the rich alone and concentrate on making the pie larger. More of everything means a higher standard of living for everybody. The forgotten part of the argument is that capital should be able to find its way to its most productive use. New businesses are formed when rich people sell assets and convert them into cash to finance a start-up. These rich people are much more likely to sell an asset when the tax on the gain is 15% than when it is 40%. It's a very simple argument but most people miss it."

"Dad, I thought you were going on forever, and it did take a couple of paragraphs to make your point. I think you're right. The concentration should be on making the pie larger. Would you advocate taking the tax on capital gains down to zero?" Stan asked.

"No. People who could afford it would play the market and do everything they could to have no income except for capital gains, placing the burden for running the government on all the other citizens. Bad idea."

"By the way, do you want me to get rid of the mentions of social engineering and fat cats and all that as I write the article?"

"Yes, you have to. I'm a well-known conservative, but no use adding pejoratives to the text. So, polish it up," Rob answered.

"Where do we go from here, Dad?"

"The section of the 1040 after Income is Adjusted Gross Income. So we have a few lines of the form devoted to reducing income prior to calculating the tax. We are at the bottom of the first page. What's the line number?"

"Line 37, and it says, This is your **adjusted gross income.** Is that important?" Stan asked.

"Yes, because if we threw out all the frills and just taxed adjusted gross income, then tax rates plummet. Incidentally, if we just taxed AGI, that's short for Adjusted Gross Income, and if we eliminated marital status, and got rid of deductions for dependents, and then poof, away goes the Alternative Minimum Tax, the dreaded AMT. We still have to get rid of standard and itemized deductions, but that's done on page two of the 1040. Incidentally, the IRS calculates the new, low rates that would result if all the changes we're advocating to the tax code were to see the light of day. They have Publication 1304, which analyzes the returns they receive. There is no intent on the part of the IRS to do our work for us, but the figures just pop up. The publication is called 'Individual Income Tax Returns' and you can buy it at the Government Printing Office."

"I suppose you have current copies?" Stan asked

"No, as a farmer I did not think I had any need for these annual publications but we certainly can obtain them. I know a professor who tracks that stuff. By the way, it's IRS publication 1304."

"Well, back to the adjustments," Stan said.

"Yes, it's so easy to get sidetracked. My blood boils a bit when I get going about our tax code. The section on Adjustments, I'd say, needs serious studying. I would hope to eliminate health savings accounts, moving expenses, student loan matters, most tuitions, and so on. The major change I'd advocate would be to convert all IRAs to Roth IRAs. Use after-tax money exclusively. Allow contributions of up to $5,000 per year. Keep the penalty for early withdrawal prior to age fifty-nine and a half. And shield all activity inside the Roth, that is, no taxes on dividends and capital gains, and do not tax the distributions which can be set by the individual. After all, after-tax money was contributed."

"Sounds simple, Dad. I believe we can turn to page two of the 1040," Stan said.

"Yes, the top of page two holds my favorite topics for reform. Here we have the standard deduction and itemized deductions. If you do not have deductions in large amounts, then you claim the standard deduction. Most people who itemize own real estate. If you are a home-owner, you get to deduct the interest portion of your mortgage payments as well as the property tax that you pay. And notice the unfairness. People who own houses usually are better off than people who rent. Most renters have never been able to come up with the down payment required to get into the housing market. Renters, therefore, have nothing to deduct. So it's a case of home owners being subsidized by renters. I would have thought that the Lefties, the great supporters of the less wealthy, would have jumped on the inequity and killed it off before it made it through the Ways and Means Committee. But that was not to be the case. I hate to be so cynical! Our brave Lefties counted up the number of home-owners in their districts and decided that they might get voted out of office if they did not support this great boondoggle. Better let the renters support the home-owners than risk losing an election."

"Dad, you're getting excited and you might not be at your best in that state," Stan said to his father.

"You're right, as usual. Here are the data that the IRS has calculated for us, inadvertently. If you tax only AGI, then this table holds the tax rate required for individuals so that income to the Treasury remains the same." With that, Rob handed Stan a sheet of paper. He asked, "Do you suppose that Claudia can put this in a small table?"

Adjusted Gross Income	Percentage of AGI Paid in Taxes
Under $10,000	3.3
$10,000 to $20,000	2.1
$20,000 to $30,000	3.9
$30,000 to $40,000	5.5
$40,000 to $50,000	6.8
$50,000 to $60,000	7.7
$60,000 to $70,000	8.4
$70,000 to $80,000	8.7
$80,000 to $90,000	9.2
$90,000 to $100,000	9.9
$100,000 to $125,000	11.3
$125,000 to $150,000	13.3
$150,000 to $175,000	14.5
$175,000 to $200,000	15.8
$200,000 to $300,000	18.1
$300,000 to $400,000	21.1
$400,000 to $500,000	22.8
$500,000 to $1,000,000	23.6
$1,000,000 and above	22.5

"I like what I see. Just calculate your AGI and pay the percentage indicated and forget the remainder of the 1040. I think people would go for it," Stan said.

"Do you think you could smooth out the curve?" Rob asked. "For instance, the percentage of tax on incomes of $10,000 is higher than on incomes of $20,000. It just turned out that way."

"We can do that, Dad, and we'll make the top rate 25%, as Secretary Mellon suggested."

"Whenever I show the plan to other persons, they like this feature. Start at line seven of the 1040, get to the bottom of the first page, far enough to calculate your AGI, and you're done for the year. Take out your calculator, find the percentage of AGI that you owe, write the check and send if off. Voila!!

"Do you think the simplicity of your plan will scare them off in Washington?" Stan asked.

"It would strike terror in the hearts of most elected officials. Imagine, a tax code that everybody understood," Rob said

"And in the hearts of all the employees at the IRS who depend on the complexity of the code for their jobs," Stan added.

A TAX CODE YOU MIGHT LIKE
PART 3

Rob and Stan were each holding a copy of the 1040 form. Rob pointed to the top of page two of the 1040. "This is the part I enjoy discussing, Stan. Hanky-panky occurs on page two of the 1040 far more often than it does on page one. To get started on this page, you must decide on the dollar amount of your legal deductions. If they are over a certain amount, say $5,500, then it makes sense to itemize them. If not, take the standard deduction. The tax code writers have assumed that most people have at least a few deductions and they allow them to reduce taxable income whether or not they could come up with a list of deductions totaling the amount of the standard deduction."

"That's what Claudia and I do. We have always taken the standard deduction and may for the remainder of our lives. It's not a bad deal."

"But if we could get rid of the concept, tax rates would fall," Rob said.

"What else shows up when people start itemizing?" Stan asked.

"An important one is the deduction for charitable contributions. As long as you can establish a market value for the gift, then I have no problem. The pledge to your church, the checks to various do-good organizations, all fine. The games get played when the value of the contribution is determined by a third party, not by a cancelled check. A person on the faculty with whom I worked closely would swear to the truth of this story. A woman was given a great deal of furniture from her parent's house when the parents decided to give up the large family home and move into a condominium. The excess pieces of furniture went into her garage and her car went on the street. Each year she would give a piece or two to a charitable organization, which organization would price out the gift and mail this woman a receipt. She never knew the final disposition of the furniture, but the receipt was part of her stack of papers that went to her tax preparer. No question that the amount ended up as a deduction on her Schedule A," Rob said.

"It seems to me," Stan said, "that Schedule A is the place where you record high medical expenses and personal losses such as your house being blown a mile or two up river by a hurricane. What to do in those cases?"

"You're right, Stan. If these deductions could be eliminated, then insurance companies would design a policy to assist in the event of a catastrophe in your life. The disaster could come as a medical problem, or in the form of a lawsuit, or your house burning to the ground, and so on. A blanket policy covering disasters is the answer and insurance companies would rise to the occasion. They would eat up the new business."

"Dad, you have gone after Schedule A, where itemized deductions are listed, but you only tore into the tax break that homeowners get with their mortgage interest and the concept of charitable contributions that take the form of something other than cash. That's not a great deal. Anything else, Dad?"

"Well, remember that I'm eliminating Schedule A in its entirety and with it goes deducting state income tax, home mortgage interest, property tax, moving expenses, various business expenses and high medical expenses. As a replacement, I'm suggesting that the insurance industry get into the business of selling a policy to cover disasters. It's a good trade-off. What we have currently, Stan, is madness. Each of us as citizens of the United States has a responsibility to maintain the operation of the government. Let the citizens, through their representatives, design a tax system that raises enough money to allow for the operation of the government. Simply taxing AGI, as I've outlined here, is one such system, certainly not the only one. Under our current system, if your charitable contributions go up, your responsibility to operate the government goes down. If you move into a larger house that carries a larger mortgage, your responsibility for the operation of the government also goes down. Same when you make a large contribution to your IRA. It's all madness. There is no connection between charitable contributions, home mortgage interest, contributions to an IRA and one's responsibility to maintain the operation of the government. I have no idea where all that nonsense came from. Elected officials on the loose are dangerous."

"Dad, you're overheating again. Let's get back to the 1040. We're on page two right now."

"I'd like to eliminate the major scandal of page two, and it's the so-called Earned Income Credit. Never was a greater piece of chicanery foisted off on the American people. It is alive for one reason: and that is if you qualify for the program, you know it in detail. If you don't qualify for it, chances are that you don't know it exists. That's another fault of having tax preparers. With a tax preparer, you get your documents back on the seventh or eighth of April, you sign them where indicated, write a check to the Treasury, and take the envelope to the Post Office. You don't even have to address the envelope. The tax preparer does that for you."

"Well, Dad, explain this awful Earned Income Credit to me, please."

"It presumes that work makes sense and that if you do not earn too much then the government will give you a credit, thereby reducing your taxes, or it might even give you a large credit that comes in the form of a refund, simply a check in the mail. The problem with the program is that it can be worked easily by anyone with half a brain."

"That must be the interesting part, the way the program is gamed," Stan said.

"Yes, that's the fascinating part. It takes only a few brain cells to mount an assault on all other taxpayers. First, there must be children involved. One, two or more children qualify the applicant for claiming the credit. Then there must be approximately the correct amount of income. If you receive too much in wages, then you don't qualify for the program. Don't think for one minute that the 1040 booklet is not studied in detail by the applicants. You can start with a family of three or four children. Husband and wife do not file using their married status. They each file as head of household and split the children among them. She uses her maiden name. If they filed as a married couple, there would be only one refund check. But splitting up so that each can file as head of household, and dividing the children, produces two checks, not doubling the take but generating a sum vastly more rewarding than a single check. It turns out that working too much reduces the amount of the credit so each partner works the amount that will produce the maximum credit. The most rewarding income for each might be $17,000 per year so that the credit reaches $4,500 each; that produces $9,000 in cash, tax free, returned to the couple a few weeks after filing their tax returns. How about that for redistribution of wealth?"

` "I wonder if Claudia and I can qualify," Stan asked.

"No children and I would guess too much income, even though you're unemployed," Rob answered.

"What have you in the way of amounts?" Stan asked.

"The bulk numbers are the best. They show you the enormity of the scam being perpetrated on the American people. These are not the most recent amounts. The IRS must spend a couple of years analyzing data before it is able to publish results." Rob said.

"Here's the table I put together and it discusses the two forms of the Earned Income Credit. Because the program is intended to aid families with children, you would think that a check every other week would make sense. A check every other week helps a family put food on the table and clothes on the kids' backs. But the writers of the tax code couldn't let it go at that. They also made it possible to take the credit in one check in April or May. How you feed and clothe kids during the other eleven months of the year is not explained." (The Advanced Earned Income Credit portion of the program was done away with in 2009, perhaps for lack of popularity.)

Rob paused as Stan examined the paper he had handed him with the data. It was short. Stan noticed that the money advanced over the year with the parent's paycheck was called Advanced Earned Income Credit, while the lump sum distribution was simply, Earned Income Credit. Each had a line devoted to it on page two of the 1040. Rob had noted in his writing that the data was taken from the 2006 issue of booklet 1304. Rob had written in the margin, "Most recent publication," and dated his note 21 July 2009.

	Advanced Earned Income Credit	Lump Sum Earned Income Credit
Number of filers	129,134	23,042,200
Amount distributed	$62,149,000	$44,387,566,000

Rob waited until his son had digested the amounts, and then said, "Divide forty-four billion dollars by twenty-three million applicants and you get about two thousand dollars per person who files for the credit. That's the average. The applicants who get the nine thousand dollars go to Disney Land or buy an up-dated used car. Feeding the children and buying them shoes has long since been forgotten."

"What's your cure in this case?" Stan asked.

"If the government thought it was imperative to have the program, then leave out the Lump Sum part of it. Force the users to use the bi-weekly method. That could reduce the size of the program and make people work a forty-hour week. Nothing wrong with that. And while we are examining amounts, divide twenty-three million applicants for the Lump Sum distribution by one hundred twenty-nine thousand applicants for the distribution over the course of the year and you get one hundred seventy-eight. So for each tax filer who does the check every other week, there are one hundred seventy-eight tax filers who go for the lump sum. It's a tragedy and a racket."

"I assume that in the back of your mind you would like to abolish both programs. Is that correct?" Stan asked

"Yes, of course. Note that we are dealing with people who are employed. It's one of the qualifications to get into the program. In many cases these individuals have only to increase the number of hours worked to earn more than the program allows."

"O.K., Dad, I'm putting the Earned Income Credit in the scrap heap when I write the article. Could that have been your intent all along?"

"Yes, I suppose so. You have read the inner chambers of my mind. I want to get this tax code down to the essentials. If you eliminate marital status, personal exemptions for yourself and the people you claim as dependents and then follow by eliminating the standard and itemized deductions, you've gone a long way toward purifying the tax code. Notice that the tax rates have plummeted, that the marriage penalty has evaporated, that small families are not subsidizing large families, that home owners are not being supported by renters, and lastly, the great achievement, it's goodbye to the Alternative Minimum Tax. This AMT was put in place to catch those taxpayers who could, in a legal fashion, shield too much income. The difficulty is that over the years, as incomes have risen, the AMT has caught ever more taxpayers in its net and that as a class these taxpayers now contribute a fair amount to the Treasury. So the Congress is not able to eliminate it, as much as it may want to, because the lost revenue should be replaced and there is no obvious way to accomplish that."

"Dad, you're probably thinking that it serves the Congress right. Is that the case?"

"Yes, if my tax code had been in place all along the situation would never have arisen. It is impossible to claim too many exemptions to your taxable income as you fill out the 1040 when you can't list any exemptions because there is no Schedule A in my version of the code."

"I think you've made a fine contribution by eliminating the Alternative Minimum Tax. Even I have heard complaints, or at least I'm aware that there are complaints about it," Stan said.

"There's more on page two that we haven't discussed. Look at the middle of the page and you find credits galore. The tax code invades all the corners of our national life. We have credits for child care, for the elderly, for education, for retirement savings, you name it. If these matters deserve addressing, let them be taken up in the various departments such as Health and Human Services, Education, and so on. Why is it necessary to reduce one's obligation to pay for the operation of the federal government simply because one tends to normal social duties, such as child care, tending to the needs of the elderly, and education?"

"Dad, you're big on discharging one's obligations, aren't you?"

"Yes, I am. The common outlook is to reduce to the minimum the amount paid in taxes without any regard for one's duty. Take the case of the municipal bond. The federal government permits the sale of bonds by municipalities and states whose interest income is tax free if the bondholder lives in the state where the bond originates. Would somebody explain that to me? The regulation permits local jurisdictions to sell bonds at a lower interest rate than the taxable bonds, such as corporate bonds. But if you are rich, you can put all your wealth into municipal bonds and reduce your obligation to run the country."

"What's your cure to that, Dad?"

"Well, it's obvious. Make all new municipal bonds taxable and allow all old municipal bonds to keep their tax-free status. Over time the old bonds would vanish. Municipalities would have to pay more to finance their projects in the future. They would have to increase interest rates to attract investors. That would be the consequence."

"Dad, you've done enough damage for the present. I know you have something to say about the federal estate tax so why don't we go to that? This paper can't be so long that no one will read it," Stan said.

"Thanks, Stan. Let's define terms first. When a person dies an estate is created and all assets and liabilities are placed in it. The executors sort out matters and with the guidance of lawyers and judges they disburse the assets after having paid off the liabilities. Depending on the value of the estate, either there is no tax to pay, or if the net value of the estate is over the minimum, there is money owed to the Treasury. The size of an estate at which a tax is due seems to vary every year. The other obligation we hear about is an inheritance tax. This differs from an estate tax in that it is paid by an inheritor after the estate has distributed its assets. Of the fifty states and the District of Columbia, twenty-four have an estate tax; six have an inheritance tax, and two, New Jersey and Maryland, have both. It's not wise to die in either of those states."

"Dad, does the federal government have an inheritance tax?" Stan asked.

"No, the feds limit themselves to an estate tax, and I would eliminate it."

"That doesn't surprise me one bit, Dad."

"Well, the estate tax generates only a little over one percent of what comes to the Treasury each year. So eliminating it is not a big deal. I have to add that the commerce generated by the elimination of the estate tax would be enormous and would generate all manner of new businesses, which, in turn, would start a new flow of tax returns to the Treasury. I must add that when I advocate the elimination of the estate tax, I'm including the elimination of the gift tax."

"Dad, there won't be any tax law left if you had your way!"

"Yes, fewer tax laws but vastly more revenue to the Treasury. Our current set of laws reduces commercial activity."

"Am I to guess that you would eliminate taxes on corporate profits?" Stan asked.

"Of course. I'm surprised I forgot to mention that. Those taxes only contribute ten percent of the total, which would be made up by taxing only AGI. But going back to the gift tax, I would permit the unimpeded flow of capital between individuals. After you have paid the tax on your adjusted gross income, you should be free to pass on assets to others. Why wait until you die? Parents may wish to give a house to a child. A grandparent may be interested in paying for the education of grandchildren. Yet other parents might wish to finance a new business that is the brainchild of an offspring. At the moment, people with wealth spend time and money devising plans to avoid the payment of the federal estate tax. All legal activities, mind you. How much more rewarding it would be to forget about estate planners! The idea would be to distribute money during one's life time and simply write a will that expresses your wishes for the remainder."

Rob went on, exhibiting his dislike for the federal estate tax. He saw no purpose in it. With assets free to move around, finding the resting place where they could do the most good, the economy of the country would operate on a more productive schedule.

Stan asked his father whether one generation might hand off appreciated assets to the next generation in order to avoid capital gains taxes. Rob thought for a moment and said that the value at the time of the gift would accompany the gift and that if the recipient sold the gift while the donor was still alive, then the capital gains tax could be paid. Stan seemed satisfied.

Rob finished his elimination of the federal estate tax by attacking those who defended it. He launched forth. "I've seen full-page newspaper ads extolling the virtues of these taxes, as though paying them were good for you. My reaction is that anyone who wishes to send money to the Treasury after death is free to do so, but please leave the rest of us alone. We have other plans for our money."

Rob felt satisfied with himself. He concluded by saying, "Stan, all we need to do is to eliminate everything except for lines seven through twenty-two on the 1040 so we calculate our adjusted gross income, then tax that amount. The revenue to the Treasury will start at an undermined amount, but over the following few years, the revenue will climb, climb, climb."

"One last thought, Dad. How does a tax code connect to Kondratiev?"

"It's not obvious and let me say that the business cycle will not be repealed by this new code. But we want to smooth out the curves, making the recessions and depressions last for a shorter time. In other words, less pain. A tax code that involves all the citizens and that provides ample money to the Treasury would tend to keep bad times at bay. There is a direct connection to the national debt and we will talk about that next."

Page 1, IRS Form 1040. Year 2010

The top portion of the form is devoted to identifying the person filing the form along with his/her filing status and number of dependents. There are 37 lines to page 1, the first 6 of them devoted to the information above. We start with line 7.

INCOME
7   Wages, salaries, tips, etc., Attach Form(s) W-2
8a   Taxable interest. Attach Schedule B if required
 b   **Tax-exempt** interest. **Do not** include on line 8a   8b
9a   Ordinary dividends. Attach Schedule B if required
 b   Qualified dividends   9b
10   Taxable refunds, credits or offsets of state and local income taxes
11   Alimony received
12   Business income or (loss). Attach schedule C or C-EZ
13   Capital gain or (loss). Attach Schedule D if required. If not required,
       check here
14   Other gains or (losses). Attach Form 4797
15a   IRA Distributions.   15a.   15b   Taxable amount
16a   Pensions and annuities   16a   16b   Taxable amount
17   Rental real estate, royalties, partnerships, S corporations, trusts, etc.
       Attach Schedule E
18   Farm income or (loss). Attach Schedule F
19   Unemployment compensation.
20a.   Social security benefits   20a.   20a.   Taxable amount
21   Other income. List type and amount
22.   Combine the amounts in the far right column for lines 7 through 21.
       This is your **total income.**

ADJUSTED GROSS INCOME
23   Educator expenses
24   Certain business expenses of reservists, performing artists, and
       fee-basis government officials. Attach Form 2106 or 2106-EZ
25   Health savings account deduction. Attach Form 8889
26   Moving expenses. Attach Form 3903
27   One-half of self-employment tax. Attach Schedule SE
28   Self-employed SEP, SIMPLE, and qualified plans
29   Self-employed health insurance deduction
30   Penalty on early withdrawal of savings
31a   Alimony paid b Recipient's SSN
32   IRA deduction
33   Student loan interest deduction
34   Tuition and fees. Attach Form 8917
35   Domestic production activities deduction. Attach Form 8903
36   Add lines 23 through 31a and 32 through 35
37   Subtract line 36 from line 22. This is your **adjusted gross income**

Page 2

TAX AND CREDITS

38   Amount from line 37 (adjusted gross income)

39a Check if you were born before January 2, 1946,   Blind   Total checked
     Spouse was born before   January 2, 1946   Blind

40   **Itemized deductions** (from Schedule A) or your **standard deduction**

41   Subtract line 40 from line 38

42   **Exemptions.** Multiply $3,650 by the number of line 6d

43   **Taxable income** Subtract line 42 from line 41. If line 42 is more than line 41, enter 0

44   **Tax** (see instructions). Check if any tax is from **a** Form 8814 or **b** Form 4972.

45   **Alternative Minimum Tax (**see instructions). Attach Form 6251

46   Add lines 44 and 45

47   Foreign tax credit. Attach Form 1116 if required

48   Credit for child and dependent care expenses. Attach Form 2441

49   Education credits from Form 8863, line 23

50   Retirement savings contributions credit. Attach Form 8880

51   Child tax credit (see instructions)

52   Residential energy credits Attach Form 5695

53   Other credits from Form **a** 3800 **b** 8801

54   Add lines 47 through 53. These are your **total credits**

55   Subtract line 54 from line 46. Of line 54 is more than line 46, enter 0

OTHER TAXES

56   Self-employment tax. Attach Schedule SE

57   Unreported social security and Medicare tax from Form **a** 4137, **b** 8919

58   Additional tax on IRAs, other qualified retirement plans, etc. Attach Form 5329 if required

59   **a** Form(s) W-2, box 9 **b** Schedule H **c** Form 5405, line 16

60   Add lines 55 through 59. This is your **total tax**

PAYMENTS

61   Federal income tax withheld from Forms W-2 and 1099

62   2009 estimated tax payments and amount applied from 2009 return

63   Making work pay credit. Attach schedule M

64a **Earned income credit (EIC)**

  b Nontaxable combat pay election

65   Additional child tax credit. Attach Form 8812

66   American opportunity credit from Form 8863, line 14

67   First-time homebuyer credit from Form 5405, line 10

68   Amount paid with request for extension to file

69   Excess social security and Tier 1 RRTA tax withheld
70   Credit for federal tax on fuels. Attach Form 4136
71   Credits from Form **a** 2439 **b** 8839 **c** 8801 **d** 8885
72   Add lines 61, 62, 63, 64a, and 65 through 71. These are your **total payments**

REFUND
73   If line 72 is more than line 60, subtract line 60 from line 72. This is the amount you **overpaid.**74a Amount of line 73 you want **refunded to you** If Form 8888 is attached, check here
75   Amount of line 73 you want **applied to your 2011 estimated tax.** AMOUNT YOU OWE
76   **Amount you owe.** Subtract line 72 from line 60.
77   Estimated tax penalty

The balance of page 2 is saved for signatures of taxpayer and tax preparer.

NATIONAL DEBT

NATIONAL DEBT
PART 1

Rob and his son Stan were talking on the telephone, each seated in his kitchen. A few days previously, Stan had talked to his father to suggest that they might combine forces and write a piece on the federal government's debt situation. Rob thought about the matter and decided that they should indeed write such an article.

"Stan," Rob said, "it will be a short piece and it should dispirit you, dispirit you considerably."

"Why so, Dad?"

"When you see it written out, you'll realize that it's all bad news, offering little hope for improvement," Rob answered.

"Before someone hires me to work on a newspaper once again and shuts down our opportunity for writing articles together, let's get to it," Stan said.

Rob and Stan met at the small office at the university that Rob used. He was enjoying a light load of teaching and guiding students through their doctoral dissertations.

"Let me start here, Stan. We can go to the Congressional Budget Office for our data. A rough approximation is all we need. Of course when they do their forecasts, all they have are rough approximations. The future is clouded, after all."

"What's our first piece of data?" Stan asked.

"I would say the annual budget deficit. It's scary. Here on table 1 (Rob held up a publication of the CBO titled 'The Budget and Economic Outlook, An Update') you see on page 2, table 1-1, that the deficit for 2009 is listed at $1,587 billions, or $1.587 trillion and that increases the public debt from $5,803 billions in 2008 to $7,612 billions in 2009. That's an enormous leap."

Stan made a calculation on a notepad. "You realize," Stan said, "that the difference between $5,803 billions and $7,612 billions is $1,809 billion, and not $1,587 billion?"

"Yes. I did, but couldn't account for it. Let's jus say that we have a rounding error on our hands."

"I'll research the matter, or let Claudia do it. She's good at that sort of thing. By the way, we have to define our terms, Dad. Go ahead and dictate them to me and I'll be certain to include them in the article."

"Good point. Debt held by the public represents the sum of the bonds, notes and bills issued by the Treasury and held by the public world-wide. We can call it the Public Debt, as I said, and at the end of fiscal year 2009 the amount was $7.612 trillions."

"And GDP," Stan said, "was over fourteen trillion dollars at the time, so the Public Debt was about half of GDP."

"That's right, and climbing," Rob said. "I've always thought interest on the debt was more significant than the debt itself. Statisticians enjoy expressing large amounts of anything, including debt, as a percentage of Gross Domestic Product, and while those are interesting associations, the important relationship is between the debt and the size of the budget. The interest on the debt is edging up and as it does, it crowds out all other programs. One way to reduce interest payments is to pay down the debt, an unlikely event surely. Another way to reduce interest payments—this method doesn't reduce the debt, it just reduces the immediate effects of it—is for the Treasury to buy back bonds that pay high interest and substitute for them bonds that pay low interest, and you can do that because interest rates fluctuate over time."

"Dad, you've thought this through. I'm running you for Secretary of the Treasury."

"Thanks, Stan. But if you make the swaps I just mentioned, short-term bonds that earn low interest payments for the holder versus long-term ones that earn high interest payments, you find that most of your debt matures in the near future, instead of having it spread out over thirty years and a Secretary of the Treasury would not enjoy being in that position. What to do when interest rates shoot up and a large portion of the debt matures and must be refinanced?" They paused for a while as Stan completed his notes.

"So much for the Public Debt. Let's move on to the Government Debt," Stan said. Rob picked up immediately. "Before we move on, let me read to you from an article in the *Journal* dated 20 June 2010. You know I clip out material when I feel I'll have a use for it. This appears on page A15 It is written by Alan Greenspan. He's discussing the debt and he says, and I quote, 'Despite the surge in federal debt to the public during the past 18 months—to $8.6 trillion from $5.5 trillion—inflation and long term interest rates, the typical symptoms of fiscal excess, have remained remarkably subdued. This is regrettable because it is fostering a sense of complacency that can have dire consequences.' Note that he's very careful to identify these sums as the 'federal debt to the public' so I gather that he's not including those pesky IOUs that we'll get into," Rob concluded.

"You were headed in the direction of the government debt," Stan continued, "when you gave me the quote from Mr. Greenspan. I suppose you were going to point out that when the amount collected in Social Security taxes exceeds the amount required to pay benefits, the amount left over goes to the Treasury where it is spent to make the budget deficit smaller than it would be otherwise."

"I suppose refunding the surplus would be a difficult proposition,"

Rob said. He paused, then said, "As an alternative, the government might have gone into the open market and purchased an assortment of Treasury bonds and thereby saved that surplus to pay benefits for the retiring baby boomers at some later date. Or the congress could also have cut the Social Security tax rate to eliminate the surplus."

"I wonder why the government did not save that surplus?" Stan asked.

"The politicians would rather give themselves credit for reducing the deficit than thinking about the long-term solvency of the Social Security system," Rob answered.

Stan added to his father's argument. "I can see that if spending the Social Security surplus provided a temporary budget surplus, let's say one that lasted two or three years, then spending the money for deficit reduction is far too tempting. We have budget surpluses so rarely that it might be asking too much from elected officials to deny themselves the pleasure. Just think of the photo ops as senators made the announcements for the evening news."

"Practically irresistible," Rob said. "I recall watching the news on those days a few years back when the balancing of the budget was announced. I think the event took place during President Clinton's second term. Of course, the press did not bring up the matter of using the Social Security surplus."

"Why not?" Stan asked.

"I can think of two reasons," Rob answered. "The first is that the reporters present did not understand the issue or the mechanics of it and the second might be that those reporters that understood the arithmetic did not wish to spoil the politicians' party."

"I can imagine that if a reporter embarrasses a senator publicly, the senator will cease to be a source of news," Stan said.

"Amen, Son. So why don't you write down that the Government Debt is the sum of all the surplus funds that have been spent by the Treasury in order to keep deficits low."

"OK," Stan said. "But I don't understand how these funds come to the government in the first place."

"When the tax or the contribution is larger than the amount required to cover the distribution, that's the general rule. We already have the example of Social Security, but you can add to that military retirements, federal employee retirements and Medicare. At times the income has been greater than the funds required to discharge the obligations with the result that a surplus shows up that can be shifted to the Treasury to pay bills."

"You're telling me, Dad, that the Treasury grabs these excess funds and spends them?"

"Yes, but they do make a bookkeeping entry of the transaction. If in a given year there is an excess of $50 billions collected in Social Security taxes, then an IOU is printed and placed in a four-draw file cabinet in a federal office building located in Parkersburg, West Virginia. This IOU is a record of the transaction but it has no value. Let me pass a hypothetical IOU in front of you so you can determine its value."

"Are these trick questions, Dad?"

"No, I don't ask trick questions, particularly of my only son. Here's the first test. If you are a functionary at the Social Security Administration, could you take this IOU and use it to pay benefits?"

"No, of course not. IOUs have no value until you collect on them."

"And how would you collect on them?"

"You can't, except by selling Treasury bonds, but you could do that with or without an IOU. They are irrelevant; the money's been spent."

"That's exactly the point, Stan. The money was received, sent to the Treasury and spent. The IOU is a record of that transaction."

"Are there people in Washington who think you can spend the same dollar twice?" Stan asked.

"Evidently. You spend it once to pay bills at the Treasury, then you print an IOU and allow it to age in a four-drawer file cabinet in West Virginia, and by some magic it gains value as it sits there so that it can be used again to pay benefits."

"That's brilliant, Dad. Claudia and I could have used that scheme when we were paying down our credit card debt."

"If you had tried it, or some version of it, you might have won a term in the local jail," Rob said.

They were silent for a moment, and then Stan asked his father, "Are these IOUs interest-bearing in some way?" Rob answered, "Yes, but the interest is paid by printing another IOU. It's a completely meaningless although harmless transaction.

The cost to the government is one sheet of 8-1/2" X 11" paper plus a little ink to operate the laser printer."

"Give me the bad news, Dad. What's the size of the Government Debt?"

"I can't tell. It moves too fast. About ten years ago, on a Thursday, I walked into the Federal Reserve building. It's on 20th and Constitution, right off the Mall, across from the Vietnam Memorial. Turns out that Thursday was the day of the week that the public was admitted to the library. By the way, there is a fine collection of small landscape paintings on the walls, all by American artists. Anyway, while there, I managed to ask for and receive a list of the government's trust funds. There were 162 of them listed on the printout I received. Those containing the largest sum of IOUs were Social Security, Medicare, military retirement, and federal employee retirement. I can't recall the sum. I suppose we could estimate that the Government Debt is about five to seven trillion dollars by now. Let us add the Government Debt to the Public Debt to arrive at the National Debt. We must be nearing fourteen trillion dollars by now."

"And the interest as a budget item?" Stan asked.

"I think it's about three hundred billion per year, a little over ten percent of the budget."

"Where did you find that figure, Dad?"

"I went to Historical tables of the Federal Budget. It's prepared by the Office of Management and Budget. It's in or near the While House."

"I take it that the amount you gave me does not include the IOUs that are generated to cover the interest on those already existing IOUs"

"That's right, Stan. The entry in the table is for 'net interest' and I assume that the amount does not cover those additional IOUs generated in Parkersburg, West Virginia. Note that I'm assuming. The document is not clear on the matter. The people in the White House don't define their terms. They may not know the definitions of them"

Rob and Stan assembled their papers and books. Stan told his father that he would start putting together the material and show it to Claudia. If there were graphs, Stan would ask her to help in organizing them and placing them in the appropriate place in the document. Claudia was a master at that sort of thing.

Claudia's first question to her husband was, "How do we stop this bleeding?" Stan had no answer except to say that the government might curtail spending. "I don't know why they don't," Claudia said. "Your newspaper had no hesitancy in letting you go when their revenues fell off," Claudia added.

"I'll put the question to Father and report back," Stan said.

Claudia was not finished. "It should be so self-evident. We could write up our experience with debt on a couple of pages. The concept is the same. All one needs to do is add nine zeros to our amounts." It annoyed Stan that his wife knew the number of zeros to add without consulting tables.

Two days later, Rob and Stan met for lunch at the cafeteria before they repaired to Rob's office. Stan related Claudia's comments to Rob, and particularly her question of what to do about the piling on of debt.

Rob looked across the room and thought for a minute. "We send the wrong people to Washington," he said. "In fact, we send the wrong people to most state capitols." Stan paused and he knew that his father would be adding to the theme in a moment.

He chimed in soon enough. "Campaigns are a market place for ideas and voters enjoy comparing the ideas that candidates put forth. Only rarely is there a price tag associated with an idea. As an example, a candidate can be for or against abortion, which program is hardly reflected in the federal budget. Alternately, a candidate can be for or against the war in Iraq, which has cost the country thousands of lives and hundreds of billions of dollars. Very few voters evaluate the cost of either abortion or a new war. They vote on the issue without regard to its cost. For the most part people vote their prejudices. People call themselves Republicans or Democrats on the basis of the prejudices they have amassed over the years."

"You would think that over-spending would not pass any test of logic and that neither Republicans nor Democrats would advocate the practice," Stan said.

"Yes, you would think so," Rob answered. "A real problem about over-spending is that it carries no pain at the beginning, exactly the same way that running up a balance on your credit card is not painful at the start. There are no consequences at first. Later on, toward the end, when the people who have been extending you credit want their money back, that's when the pain sets in. It is starting to happen to the United States. Countries that have bought our Treasury bonds with their export earnings are beginning to get nervous, just as your credit card companies did."

Rob said, "It may appear that I'm changing the topic, but trust me, I'm still answering your question. What can be done about the spending? I think we will need a catastrophic event in order to change people's thinking. Without it, voters will not concern themselves first and foremost with the cost of legislation and elected officials will continue to promote expensive new programs that, in their opinion, will please constituents and result in re-election. So the behavior of voters and their representatives must change in fundamental ways. You don't do that without an event so large that the thinking of the population is altered."

"You have something in mind?" Stan asked his father.

"Let's say that the snow and ice sheet covering Greenland melted with the result that all this cold water flowed into the North Atlantic. The warming effect that the Gulf Stream now has on Northern Europe might vanish. Iceland, England, Ireland, Norway, Sweden, Denmark, Holland, Belgium, Northern France might become uninhabitable. Perhaps there are a hundred million people living in those countries; what to do with them? They would have to be resettled. Now that would get the world's attention. There would no longer be a debate about global warming. That's the power of a catastrophic event."

"Any chance that could happen?" Stan asked.

"Unlikely, but it could happen. A catastrophic event took place in Germany after World War I. There was a case of runaway inflation and the mark lost all its value. The various levels of government, manufacturing, retail sales, all those activities ground to a halt. All savings were wiped out. The German governments seventy-five years after that event are still sensitive to setting off inflation. Can you imagine what would happen if the dollar lost all value?"

"Not really. Inflation is the friend of people who carry debt. Claudia and I could have used a dose of it a couple of years ago, but you are right, it's too punishing for the entire system and all its inhabitants."

"And that's why our trading partners are worried. After the Chinese, I think that Japan and the oil exporters in the Middle East are next on the list of large owners of our Treasury bonds. Wouldn't you hate to be the finance minister of China and watch your nearly trillion dollars of Treasury bonds melt away in purchasing power?"

"Is it a problem that we can solve?" Stan asked.

"As I said, elect a new group of legislators, but get them to pay attention to spending and lose interest in new social programs that cost a fortune. In any event, we may need a catastrophic event such as occurred in Germany in the 1920s."

"The cure can only come after we have been punished as a nation, is that it?" Stan asked.

"Yes, unfortunately. Wouldn't it be convenient if we could modify our nation's behavior without a catastrophic event? I'll answer my own question. It would be marvelous if we got religion on financial matters without needing the curative powers of a catastrophic event. But it has not happened elsewhere and there is no reason that it will happen here."

"So you think we are on the way to hyperinflation?"

Rob thought for a moment. "I've not been asked the question before but let me tell you confidentially that the possibility is out there, a large, black cloud gathering in size and moving closer, that threatens to destroy the best parts of the United States." Rob paused and then added, "I haven't sold the ten acres with the two small houses."

Stan was silent for a moment, gathering his thoughts. "Dad, why don't you make contact with Mr. Greenspan? I know you've met him."

"Yes, at conferences, in a crowded room. What were you thinking of?"

"Could you ask him his views on the debt and the chances of repaying a good portion of it?"

NATIONAL DEBT
PART 2

Stan and his father, Rob, had been distracted and had not worked diligently on the project of writing their article on debt. Stan had discovered that writing fiction was absorbing and Rob was kept busy on projects around the house that Rose felt were urgent. Both men knew they had to get on with the project.

Rob dialed his son. "You remember the crisis in Greece?" Rob asked Stan.

"Yes indeed. I would place it in the year 2010, or thereabouts," Stan answered.

"2010 is correct. The lesson was and remains the same, that you can't overspend forever," Rob said.

"You are taking the risk of repeating yourself," Stan said. "We may have been through some of this before."

"That's true, but it's worth driving home the point. Did we go over this concept in our first pass at writing an article on debt?"

"Yes, you did touch on the matter, but no harm in a little repetition, as you say," Stan said. They were talking from their respective telephones, both sitting in their kitchen and drinking coffee. Claudia was at work, but Rose was at the table with Rob. "Your mother wants to say good morning to you," Rob announced.

"Are you two concocting plans?" Rose asked.

"Yes. Dad thinks we should get back to work and discuss the debt taken on by various governments, our federal government in particular, and make the point that while some debt is acceptable, more debt leads to disaster in the end. I think that sums up his point."

"Another article written jointly?" Rose asked

"Yes. We can break it into segments and hope my former newspaper will publish it in serial form. I think Dad wants to start with the debt crisis that seized Greece in 2010."

Rob and Stan met in Rob's small office. It was mid-morning and they knew they would organize the article before heading for the student union and lunch.

"My point is always the same," Rob said. "Massive debt makes it difficult for the brain to operate and important people find that they can't think of anything except how to get out of the fix that either they or their predecessors got them into."

"When you brought up the matter before, you were talking mostly about executives at corporations that were wallowing in debt. You'll have to find a new emphasis to keep our article interesting," Stan said.

"It may be better to keep our article frightening than interesting, although I agree with you in general," Rob went on. "In any event, the ramifications of government debt are different from those caused by corporate debt. At corporations, after all, when conditions are favorable, the board of directors can elect to sell shares in the corporation, raise cash, and pay off debt. Governments, on the other hand, can only reduce their debt by cutting spending or increasing taxes. Reducing spending hurts some of the electorate and increasing taxation has the same effect, perhaps on another segment. Sometimes increasing taxation does not bring in more revenue. You and I have discussed the tax cuts that Andrew Mellon asked for, the tax cuts by Presidents Kennedy and Reagan and how they all resulted in additional revenue to the Treasury. Those events are powerful lessons. And while we are at it, I have read that President Andrew Jackson paid off the national debt in 1835, the only time in the history of the republic that the condition has existed, so it can be done. Thank goodness for that event. It can be done."

"It sounds appealing, to be out of debt," Stan said, "but I can think of situations in which there exists a need for Treasury bonds."

"I'll let you write that paragraph, Stan. I could think of a few cases but I feel it's a topic you've explored already. Give me some examples," Rob asked.

"Think of life insurance companies, Dad. For the most part they do not adjust over time either the premium or the amount they pay out on maturity of the policy so the long-term Treasuries match their requirements. Life insurance companies are pleased to have long-term Treasuries to turn to."

"That's a good example, Stan."

"Then you have municipalities, school districts, counties, and plenty of other governmental entities who receive a slug of tax money, perhaps twice a year, and they have to park it in a safe place and what better solution than to buy Treasuries.?"

"Well thought through, Stan. It's obvious that inflation is disastrous. One or two percent per year is acceptable, but when you hit five percent, someone has to put on the brakes and that's the Fed, driving up the interest rates, of course slowing down the economy," Rob said.

"Inflation and debt seem to be joined at the hip," Stan observed. "Sometime the connection is not obvious," Rob added.

Stan said, "There's an element of unfairness. The federal government can borrow and spend and bring on inflation but then anyone holding cash or bonds gets burned. You sit there helpless and watch your assets vaporize."

Rob countered, "Some people do well in inflationary times and you must make that point in your segment of the article. If you are paying down a mortgage or if you happen to be the U.S. Treasury, heavily in debt, you see your difficulties easing."

Both Stan and Rob had been taking notes as they spoke. Nearly in unison they stood up and said, "Lunch."

When seated and spooning their vegetable soup, Stan asked his father, "Do you think the debt the Greek nation has taken on will ever be repaid?"

"I don't believe so, Stan. The Greek government will trim its budget, perhaps reaching a surplus for a year or two, and then they will repudiate their debt. In the process they will inherit the cleanest balance sheet among the European nations. They will bow out of the Euro zone and the new drachma will appear."

"Will anyone in his right mind lay out money to buy the new Greek bonds?" Stan asked.

"There is the P.T. Barnum aspect, to the effect that a sucker is born every minute, but more than that there are always people who need to earn a little interest. Of course, people have sieve-like memories. Argentina defaulted on a portion of its debt, as did Russia. But these countries still function in international markets. Argentina has beef and wine to sell. Russia is probably the largest exporter of oil and natural gas. Repudiation of debt is a fact of life. We see it on a small scale when individuals declare bankruptcy and on a larger scale when a corporation goes through the same process. Now we are seeing municipalities, counties, perhaps several states and even countries all following the same path."

"Well, those are sobering thoughts, Dad. What do you think about the U.S.?"

"It is too soon to tell whether we will repudiate. Certainly we will not pay off our debt," Rob said.

"What's certain about that?" Stan asked.

"The current thinking on the topic is that you need only grow the economy faster than you take on debt. Economists speak of the ratio of debt to Gross Domestic Product. We were at 30% or so for a while but now that's passed beyond 60%. Perhaps we've hit 100%. The call is to grow the economy, not cut spending. That's a difficult thing to do when the government consumes more and more of the money available. By the way, that's why I wrote a new tax code. In it you saw an opportunity to get rid of all those crazy credits and particularly the Earned Income Credit and all the deductions listed on Schedule A."

"That would be quite a victory if your new tax code were given the time of day," Stan said.

"Yes, we could clean house. You realize, of course, that we pay farmers to grow corn that is made into ethanol. Imagine using food to make fuel when you can find fuel in the ground. Anyway, we could eliminate all those agricultural subsidies," Rob said.

"It's a great way to reduce the size of the budget but let's go back to what's on the minds of elected officials."

"Good point, Stan. I get carried away and we lose focus. The elected officials, at all levels of government, are looking over their shoulders. Is there a wave of financial sanity about to break over them and sweep them out to sea? That's what they are asking."

"That's a literary analogy, Dad. I'll have to snuff it out."

"Right you are, Stan. That was a euphemism for losing an election. Elected officials at the local level are thinking about their own budgets, how to reduce spending and still provide services; at the federal level they are thinking less about bringing home the bacon. All of them are wondering how strong a signal of financial caution they have to emit in order to get elected or re-elected. I think it's that simple."

"On another topic, Dad, do you think that the Kondratiev waves have an effect on the actions of governments? Could you tie in the Greek governmental escapade with the commercial activity of that country?"

"It would be difficult. You would be required to examine all of recent history and make sense of it. As an example, the hyperinflation in Germany in the 1920s was a result of the war, while the Greek troubles were caused by years of overspending. If there is a unified theory then the author of it goes on the short list for a Nobel Prize in economics. Of course you can't get away from the fact that there was folly in the air."

"That makes it worth thinking about, Dad. It would be a great cap to your career."

"I suspect there exist connections between political and commercial activities but the connections are obscure. If they were a bit more obvious, economists would have identified them by now."

"You know that Einstein spent his final years in search of a unified theory that brought together gravitation and sunlight, good old electromagnetic radiation?" Stan asked.

"Yes, I knew that, Stan. The German physicist, Erwin Schrödinger did as well. My recollection is that they both failed at the attempt," Rob said.

"Indeed they did, but my guess is that they came close. By the way, we can be generous toward our senators and representatives. Let's say that as well as worrying about re-election they do concern themselves with overspending, that it may bring down the country," Stan said.

"Fair enough, Stan. That's a generous impulse on your part." Rob thought for a moment then said, "They did think about the topic but they didn't do anything about it."

NATIONAL DEBT
PART 3

R ob and Stan were working at a slow pace. Their excuse was that the federal agencies they had written for data were non-responsive. Furthermore they

complained to one another that they had no influence over these government bodies to get them to answer letters and send graphs, tables and data.

One evening, Claudia and Stan were at Rose and Rob's new house, invited particularly to view the collection of used furniture that had been acquired. They had finished dinner and were still at table when Rob brought up the matter of the unfinished paper on the National Debt.

"I hate to concede," Rob said, "but we may be licked."

"Perhaps a trip to Washington could fix matters," Stan said. "You should be able to visit the offices in question and oblige them to produce the information we need."

Claudia could be counted on to add her opinion. In the last few years she had become more talkative than she was when she and Stan married. Rose and Rob speculated that the economic hardships being endured by the country at large had forced her to start communicating on the sad state of affairs. She said, "You may not need additional data. You know what's going on to a close approximation. You should be able to finish your paper based on rough numbers."

"It's the professor in me, I suppose," Rob said. "Í have to get it down to the last centime."

"Can you say more, Claudia?" Stan asked.

"The entire mood of the country has to switch. Never mind the few million dollars here and there. We are talking about important people acting responsibly. Elected bodies down to the last person must change the way they do business. Governments at all levels must honor saving over spending. You're talking about a colossal shift."

"How would you bring that about?" Rose asked.

"Voters have to learn to elect the correct people. The current crop is failing us. The signs of disaster have to be stronger, I suppose. We behave now as though we could follow John Maynard Keynes forever and continue priming the pump with government programs."

Rob said, "Claudia, to be fair to Keynes, I'll tell you what he wrote on the matter but only after you've finished developing your ideas."

"Do you have his books here?" Claudia asked.

"Yes, right over there in that bookcase."

"We will be safe when an avowed spender can't get elected, when the citizenry and elected people realize that there is no answer in yet another social program. That's when sanity will return." Claudia leaned back in her chair and Stan thought that she was yielding the floor but she went on to introduce a similar idea that he had heard but his parents had not. "When we saved ourselves, I'm talking about Stan and me saving ourselves, we cut up our credit cards. We didn't owe any less, our debt didn't decrease, but we knew we were headed in the correct direction. It's similar to standing at the edge of the ocean. A couple of feet in one direction, you're in the water up to your knees. A couple of feet in the other direction, you're completely dry. Just a few feet but the difference is night and day."

"It's a nice contrast," Rob said. The mention of the ocean made him recall the first day of October five or six years ago when Claudia and Stan wanted one last swim in the ocean before fall returned in earnest. The four of them drove to a beach north of Atlantic City. It was deserted. The wind was blowing at a fair rate. Rose and Rob had no intention of going in but Claudia and Stan, holding hands, marched right in and swam up and down, not far from the water's edge. When they came out of the water, Stan put on a white sweatshirt. Claudia, facing away from Rose and Rob, removed her top and took a towel from her canvas bag. She dried her hair, face and arms. Rob remembered having said to Rose, "I wish she would turn around."

"Me too," Rose answered.

"No doubt for a different reason," Rob said.

"Yes. I want to see if she's better up front than I was at her age."

"My sweet, you have always been in the major leagues. Most valuable player, every year in fact."

"That's kind, and sexy too, Robby."

They had continued watching Claudia who dropped the towel and put on her sweatshirt. Stan had turned away and was studying the waves and the sky and clouds.

"That's the way it is with me, Robby. I'm predisposed to wanting you and when you kiss me most anywhere my whole nervous system comes to life."

Rob would recall the scene and the conversation from time to time. He knew it had nothing to do with excess spending on the part of the government but Claudia's comments on being at the edge of the ocean were right on target as far as the attitude required to bring spending under control.

Claudia went on a bit, suggesting that Rob and Stan could finish the article by exhorting the elected class to change their ways. They did not need sets and sets of data. "What might be persuasive," Claudia added, "would be the list of savings you wanted to make in the budget. Say go back five years and use those budgetary figures as the new set for the current or coming year."

Rob thought a minute and gave his reactions. "All elected officials say they will cut spending and end waste in government. I notice they are not specific. I would reduce in size the Energy Department, same with Education and Commerce. Those departments might be dropped after a thorough study."

"And plenty of jobs would go out the window," Stan observed. "All hell would break loose; strikes, marches, and all that."

"Give someone something and it's terribly difficult to take it away," Rose said.

"Particularly when it's that person's livelihood," Rob said. "That may be why politicians refrain from providing details on how they would cut spending."

They fell silent, and then Rose said, "If it gets done it will be when no other solution is at hand. That is, the government is out of money and not able to borrow anymore."

"One possibility," Rob said. "is to cut back, cut programs and wages in an attempt to save jobs and bank on attrition to cut the work force."

Rose put her hand on her husband's arm and asked, "Didn't you write a paper on this whole business of debt, I would guess about six years ago?"

"Yes, I did," Rob answered. "It was titled *Perplexities in Debt Financing,*" and I was not able to get it published."

"I wasn't about to bring that up," Rose said.

"No matter. The people to whom I submitted the paper said that the material wasn't sufficiently illuminating, that the points I was making were common knowledge."

"You agonized over the matter. It's been your only rejection," Rose said.

"Do you still have a copy of it?" Stan asked.

"Yes, I couldn't throw it away. It's part of me by now."

"Can you find the copy and let us read it?" Stan asked.

"Yes, but I don't have to. I can give you the salient points any moment you wish."

"What's the first one?" Claudia asked.

"Organizations and people that take on debt to finance projects must be careful to be on the correct side of the equation. In an inflationary environment you want to be the one who borrows and pays back interest and principal over time. As the months and years go by, the payments become easier to make. During inflationary times you never want to be the lender. You never recover the amount you have lent out. Maybe that's obvious and the editors were correct to turn down my paper."

Claudia persisted. "What followed the first point?"

"Exploring two points that are bound together by the phenomenon of inflation. The first is the challenge of maintenance and the other is the difficulty of saving for the long term, as governments ought to do to cover pension liabilities."

"Why don't you give us the big picture, Dad?" Stan asked.

"Let's start with maintenance. Look at the Interstate Highway System, or any bridge, or a tunnel. Once these projects are completed and put into use, they start requiring service, or maintenance. Eventually the item must be replaced. If you start saving for maintenance and eventual replacement, the purchasing power of the savings will decline year after year. With a project having a long life, such as a suspension bridge, the first amount of money saved, just as the project was finished, has lost most of its purchasing power over time. Legislators, knowing this, will not set up saving mechanisms and prefer to pay for maintenance on an as-needed basis year by year."

"I suppose that's acknowledged fact," Stan said. "How about governments and their long-term obligations, such as pensions?"

"Not unlike maintenance," Rob answered. "You ask employees to kick in over the years of their employment so that when they retire there is a pool of assets to pay for their retirements. The actuaries and investment managers who run these pension funds have a very difficult job. If they don't beat inflation in their returns, they end up with an underfunded pension system for the employees. All hell breaks loose, and of course that leads right into the reason for Social Security. If Social Security were a system similar to the pension funds used by the states, then there would be managers struggling to invest billions of dollars of Social Security collections to create an enormous fund to pay for the retirements of an entire population. Naturally the program has always been pay-as-you-go, the current workers paying for the retirement of the previous workers. There is no system of investment."

"Could there be one?" Stan asked.

"I don't think so," Rob said. "Dividends declared on common stocks and interest paid on bonds would come under scrutiny of the federal government making the system unworkable. Those issues are left properly to the boards of directors of corporations."

"Is inflation the reason that the federal government does not save?" Rose asked.

"I would say it's the principal reason. A contributing factor is that legislators would find projects that demanded the use of the saved funds. Legislators have learned to make promises. They find interesting new projects and make promises. That activity is more rewarding to their careers than setting money aside for a rainy day."

"Dad, the editors may have been correct. There might not be enough new material to warrant a publication," Stan said.

"But I had a clinching argument," Rob said. "It had to do with the acceptable level of government spending and the resultant debt. The argument went like this: Because inflation makes saving difficult, or impossible, governments, faced with the maintenance of so many projects that they are responsible for, must keep their spending low and debt to a small portion of GDP, so that they may borrow with ease as maintenance projects come due. I ask you, how will the federal government find the money to rebuild the bridges that span San Francisco Bay and the major rivers elsewhere? The George Washington Bridge's replacement could be a multi-billion dollar affair."

"Did you have some figures in your paper?" Claudia asked.

"Yes. You know me. Tables, graphs, amounts, and so on. I concluded that the national debt should be one quarter of GDP so that borrowing at a reasonable interest rate would be a snap. I guess we are at 100% of GDP. Debt is costly. The standard answer now is to postpone maintenance."

"Perhaps your timing was off, Dad," Claudia said. She had started calling Rob Dad as her father had died and she found no encouragement to use his first name. "Your paper is certainly topical today," she concluded.

Rob said, "I want to come back to Keynes and his 1936 book." Rob stood up and walked to his bookcase and withdrew Keynes' text. "It's titled *The General Theory of Employment, Interest and Money.*" Rob was holding a second book. He read the title, "*The Economics of John Maynard Keynes.*

It's by Dudley Dillard. He was at the University of Maryland. I think that Keynes implied that while it was acceptable to take on deficit spending during tough times, you had to pay back the funds you borrowed in good times. Dillard says the same thing. I'm on page 113. *'It is quite consistent for those who advocate loan expenditure, or deficit financing, in depression to advocate balanced budgets during boom periods.'* Even that statement by Dillard is not strong. He goes as far as balanced budgets but does not advocate paying off debt. There is no imperative about what he says. Sounds like a suggestion."

Rob snapped the book shut and said, "As you can see, there are no Keynesians. Republicans and Democrats alike borrow money to spend and neglect to pay back the amounts borrowed when the good times return. There are no elected, functioning Keynesians, if I may conclude that a true Keynesian would advocate paying back the borrowed funds. There may be a few conservative members of state legislatures, but there's no one in Washington who measured up. I remember vaguely from my days as an undergraduate that one of my professors identified a senator from Vermont by the name of George Aiken, a Republican no less, who in the middle of the 1950s, advocated continuing the agricultural subsidies that had been put in place during the Depression or World War II. Everyone went along with the idea. Eisenhower was president at the time. I've always looked at it as the crucial moment when the federal government could have gone the other way by eliminating these subsidies and starting on a serious program of debt reduction."

"Have we ever had zero national debt?" Claudia asked.

"Once. I believe it was in 1835 during Andrew Jackson's second term. He simply hated debt. I think I've mentioned this before."

"We need Jackson back," Claudia said.

Rob had another thought. "It should not be forgotten that we do not need economists to tell us what to do. Debt does not let you go. Too much debt screams at you. Italy was long thought of as the sick man of Europe because its government debt had climbed beyond Gross Domestic Product. Greece and Ireland were next. Is our turn coming? There are inevitable effects of too much debt. One is that the interest on the debt crowds out valuable programs. The second is that interest rates go up. I know that the correlation is not absolute, but in general the statement is true. And third, no one will lend to you. Do you recall that Zimbabwe ran out of space on its currency to accommodate the zeros required? It comes to that."

Stan said, "Dad, I think your point about there being no Keynesians, not in either party, is the most important point you've made so far. It makes the paper. It blows me away."

"I'm waiting for the first president to stop talking about making deficits smaller, and moving to a balanced budget. I want a president to create years of surplus and reduce the debt to a manageable level." Rob seemed to have summed up the discussion.

"Amen," Rose said.

THE
AFTERMATH

THE AFTERMATH

It was the summer of 2018. Rose and Rob were most pleased by the arrival of Claudia's daughter who was christened Rose and immediately called Rosebud. Rose doted on the child but made room for the other grandmother, Claudia's mother, whose names were Mary Elizabeth. Claudia maintained that these names were beautiful but therefore overused. Elizabeth became the middle name of Rosebud and peace was maintained in the family.

The recovery had moved by inches when it needed to gallop ahead. Kondratiev would have despaired but he would have understood. During his lifetime, the Left in the Soviet Union had seized all wealth, permitting the cream of the crop of their own politicians to use fancy cars and substantial retreats in the country. Rob and Stan discussed the anomaly of stripping the comfortable aspect from the population at large only to hand it out to the top dogs of the Communist party. What folly and what hypocrisy!

In the United States, heavy taxation where possible paid for the generous welfare programs. The Left had identified their majority of voters as the recipients of subsidized housing, ample food programs, education paid for and the near abolition of the wealthy class. The elected officials of the Left put in place all their welfare programs before starting in on the demolition of the rich. This they accomplished through taxation. These elected officials would say to one another, "The power to tax is the power to destroy." They would smile.

Once the Left held the majority in the House of Representatives and the Senate by substantial margins, and had one of their own sleeping in the White House, apparently in perpetuity, it was a simple matter to double the federal estate tax and to increase taxes on dividends, capital gains, business income and ordinary incomes as well. They had the votes to nationalize the energy industry and with that they were in absolute control. The courts fell into their hands as over time they were able to appoint to the bench judges who felt as they did—that having wealth was indecent and smashing up those who had it in vast amounts was fair play.

The Left, to its discomfort, could not devise means of having the economy grow, which they admitted would be the correct thing to do, as the population continued to expand and new jobs were always in demand. They found out, as all Socialists do, that taxing capital gains had the effect of drying up sources of venture capital, which slowed up the formation of new businesses. They had known this all along but could not believe it strongly enough to act on it.

There were side effects of bringing down the wealthy class. An unforeseen result was that theaters, museums, symphonies and operas, hospitals and churches were soon enough out of leadership and money. Previously, rich people had served on the boards of directors of these charitable organizations but over time they dropped off and local governments, if they wished to continue with the services of a hospital or a symphony orchestra, would have to petition the federal; government for funds and occasionally management. Gradually, what had been under the management of local do-gooders became part of local government, on a reduced scale in quality and size.

"It's a bland world, compared to the world I grew up in," Rob exclaimed once to Stan.

"I did enjoy the antics of the rich crowd," Stan answered. "Our paper would always cover the opening of the opera. You had photographs of women in furs and diamonds, chauffeur-driven limousines, an occasional gentleman in a top hat. I rather liked it."

"The University misses the old crown a lot," Rob carried on. "They always ran the fund raising drives. We did one for two billion once. Terrific stimulus for all of us. Now the big news takes place when the Department of Education awards us a grant."

"What brought on this class warfare?" Stan asked.

"It lives right under the surface. Plain old envy will do it," Rob answered. "There may be more to it. But say you've received a basic education and you're holding down an average job and the prospects for you are just not that grand, then you could conclude that you have been dealt a bad hand of cards and you are owed a few freebies to cheer you up, and who better to pay for these benefits than those rich people who are probably living off ill-gotten gains? Never mind that they have educated themselves very well and worked diligently over the years, never mind all that, and don't admit to your self that you never cared to study and don't work that hard at your job. Never mind any of it. They have the money. You don't. Tax them hard and pass it around."

"It probably is that simple, Dad. Lord knows Claudia and I don't feel that way, and my sister Harriet is a slave to her hospital. She deserves everything she earns." Stan changed the subject. "Do you think we'll get it back after a while, Dad? Will it be our turn?"

"Thank goodness life is cyclical. The current benefactors of all this redistribution will get tired of the grayness in their lives, the grayness everywhere. As you recall, your mother and I went to Russia a few years after the Communist regime collapsed—I think it was 1996—and the young women had led the charge. They were dressing as well as the women in Western Europe, perhaps better. From fancy hair to the latest in shoes. It was remarkable. They were saying enough of this enforced plainness. We want our share of gayety and glamour while we are young. Plenty of time to be drab later on. So yes, Stan, we will have our turn but the current majority will have to tire of what they have created."

"And when do you suppose that could take place?" Stan asked.

"All in good time. The perpetrators will have to survey the wreckage they have caused and decide that it is time to let go. Note that the Communist regimes folded without too much holding on. I guess the great mass of the functionaries were fed up with what they had created, all those concrete slabs, and calling one another comrade, and living in fear of violating the smallest rule. They must have been fed up with the whole lot of it."

They went to the student union and lunch. They walked across the campus in silence but once seated Rob had more to explore. "Let me ask you this, Stan. We can take the population as a whole and put the rich in one segment, and with them the younger crowd that feels it has a good chance of becoming rich. They know they are well educated and are on a good career track. Then we have a larger segment than the rich that represents the middle class and then after them the less well off economically."

"You mean the poor?" Stan asked.

"Yes, but I don't like to use that adjective. How about lower class economically?"

"That's fine, Dad."

"Well, whatever term we use, they sense that they will not crack through to reach the top and frankly they resent it. They wish they had more of everything."

"I'm sure, Dad, that you realize that within the two large groups you have indicated, there are plenty of subgroups. One could be rich people that favor heavy taxation on estates, contrary to what you might expect from them. And then among the poor you will find some who have no envy, carry no grudges, and wish the rich well."

"You're right, Stan. All large groups can be subdivided. I should have thrown that in. But I wanted to bring up a different group, smaller than the two we have been discussing. Let's call them the Implementers. This group is made up of well-educated, hard working people who, you would think, would associate themselves with the rich, yet they go off in the other direction. They design, support, and sometimes implement the welfare programs and make life uncomfortable for their natural allies. I simply don't understand them — the inconsistency of it all. These Implementers are doing all they can to become rich themselves and to make it big in our society, while at the same time they make life as difficult as possible for the people whose life style they are trying to emulate."

"Would you refer to these Implementers as Liberals, Dad?" Stan asked.

"To a man they are," Rob answered.

"Perhaps I can explain them," Stan volunteered. He proceeded to do that. "The fact that they exist in both camps at once, which you find bizarre, if not unacceptable, comes from having a diverse set of aspirations for the population. For themselves they want the good life if not a life of luxury. They want to make it to the top. You find them in university faculties, foundations, governmental agencies and even in business. For the poor they want access to the features in our country that give hope for moving up from poverty to the middle class. I don't think that they care whether the poor make it up a couple of rungs. They just want to know that for some it will be possible. They feel that upward mobility is made possible by actions of the government, not by any other means, and therefore they are comfortable with the notion of the government taxing the rich in order to put the necessary social programs in place."

"It interests me that these people do not want the poor to work themselves up into the middle class and even beyond," Rob interrupted.

"If they did," Stan said right away, "they would have to be on our side, cutting taxes on business profits and capital gains and even dividends. In other words, they would have to be just like us. There would be no need for the Left."

"They go too far with it, Stan. You've noticed, of course, that the former Communist countries have changed style, all except Cuba, and that the European countries that have Socialist governments have cut their programs in order to reduce spending? Margaret Thatcher made the most trenchant remark on the subject: 'In the end you run out of other people's money.' That's what we are seeing taking place in Europe, and precisely what we have done to ourselves, run up a national debt in the trillions of dollars, and to what purpose? Have the elected officials done anything more than create a dependent society?"

"Probably not," Stan answered. "Plenty of Implementers, as you call them, feel good about what they have accomplished. It's appropriate to refer to them as a group, as the Left, I think."

"Yes indeed. They are the Lefties. They are an expensive lot. At least they are not revolutionary," Rob said.

Stan fell into agreement. "Yes, they manage to get done what they aspire to accomplish without a revolution. By the way, where would Kondratiev place us on his curve at this moment?"

"I would say at the end of Recovery and at the start of Steady State. We've been through plenty on our return to a passable version of normality," Rob said to his son.

"In fifty years, when all the data on the wave we have lived through has been gathered, it will be great to compare this wave with the others we have had, particularly the Great Depression. Wouldn't it be great if Crusoe or Rosebud followed in our footsteps and had a career in Finance?"

About the Author

Fred Weekes lives in Lakewood, Washington, a city forty-five miles south of Seattle on the I-5 corridor. After a career in business and engineering he retired to writing on topics that interested him: World War II aviation, general reference, and love stories. Some of these titles are available through iUniverse. Some can be found at Amazon for reading on one's Kindle. He enjoys writing romances. They may be his favorites.

The room that Weekes writes in has a fine view of a lake. Water fowl are in abundance and an occasional heron and eagle come by.

Weekes holds degrees from the University of Pennsylvania and Catholic University of America. He prizes these as he sees no chance of earning additional degrees.